NIGHT MARSHAL

NIGHT MARSHAL

L. P. Holmes

Chivers Press • G.K. Hall & Co.
Bath, England   Thorndike, Maine USA

This Large Print edition is published by Chivers Press, England, and by G.K. Hall & Co., USA.

Published in 2001 in the U.K. by arrangement with the author, c/o Golden West Literary Agency.

Published in 2001 in the U.S. by arrangement with Golden West Literary Agency.

U.K. Hardcover   ISBN 0-7540-4407-6   (Chivers Large Print)
U.K. Softcover   ISBN 0-7540-4408-4   (Camden Large Print)
U.S. Softcover   ISBN 0-7838-9320-5   (Nightingale Series Edition)

The text of this Large Print edition is unabridged.
Other aspects of the book may vary from the original edition.

Set in 16 pt. New Times Roman.

Printed in Great Britain on acid-free paper.

British Library Cataloguing in Publication Data available

Library of Congress Cataloging-in-Publication Data

Holmes, L. P. (Llewellyn Perry), 1895–
    Night marshal / L.P. Holmes.
        p.   cm.
    ISBN 0-7838-9320-5 (lg. print : sc : alk. paper)
    1. United States marshals—Fiction. 2. Large type books.
    I. Title.
PS3515.O4448 N54   2001
813'.52—dc21
                                                        00–049883

CHAPTER ONE

The three car narrow gauge train pulled into Decker's Flat a full hour late, which put the time of its arrival a few short minutes before sunset. From the rear coach, Chris Waddell stepped down into a gust of biting air funneling off the timbered heights above. The chill struck quick and deep and he hunched his shoulders under the scanty protection of a faded denim jumper.

He was a tall man with a gauntness that touched his face, for his cheeks were drawn and his gray eyes sunken. Above a square chin his mouth was level, slightly harsh. He had the look of one who had not smiled in a long time. When he moved it was with care, holding himself almost severely erect to favor a but lately healed wound in his flank.

Other travelers left the train. Behind Waddell came a slender, supple man in the wide dark hat and long coat of the professional gambler. Except for a thin line of mustache, this was a clean-shaven one who surveyed the world with an edge of white-toothed smile and from eyes reflecting the ghost of a sardonic, reckless cynicism. He carried a small bag of luggage and his soft, calfskin boots were polished to a high gloss.

Several miners, with bundles of blankets

1

and other gear, also climbed down. These were the confirmed drifters, the restless ones, answering the lure of still another booming gold camp.

A young woman emerged from the coach ahead. She dropped from the steps with a lithe, sure ease, then moved slightly aside, turned and made some smiling remark to the conductor as he brought down a rattan valise and a canvas gripsack. She wore a short, tan coat whose turned-up collar framed a warm-skinned cleanly featured face. Her head was bare and the last glow of the afternoon sunlight awakened tawny glints in her hair. Carrying her valise and gripsack she moved quickly over to the station house and out of sight beyond it.

Decker's Flat was the high point of climb for the narrow gauge, as close as steel rails could get to Midas Hill, the gold camp which lay a good fifteen miles further back in the rugged reaches of the Bannock Mountains. Besides the weather-stained station house, the flat contained a store and warehouse and a sprawling building which was at once a bar, an eating house and a hotel of sorts. Beyond these was a stage and freight corral with feed sheds and a compound holding several burly, high-wheeled Merivale freighters, a thoroughbrace Concord stage and a mud wagon. The corral held a full complement of horses and mules and spread its sharp odors through the chilling air.

The train lurched into movement again, chuffing slowly out through a wye of tracks at the far end of the flat, where, with much creaking and squealing of wheel flanges, it reversed itself and hauled back to the station. Here a squat hand truck, stacked with fat sacks of rich concentrate, was wheeled into place and the sacks loaded into the baggage car. Each sack carried a stenciled number and an alert eyed young fellow with a sawed-off shotgun over one arm and a belt gun about his lanky middle, checked them against a list. When the last sack went through the car door he followed it in.

The conductor, carrying a fistful of papers, came out of the station house, waved an arm. The engine bell answered, draw-bars jerked and clacked and the train began to roll, heading away on its run back to the low country. It was soon gone, leaving behind the wet, penetrating breath of steam and coal smoke to vie with the odors of the freight corral. Diminished with distance came the lonely, long-running wail of its whistle.

Backed up against the station wall out of the worst of the chill air-drift, and where he might soak up the last touch of the dying sunlight, Chris Waddell watched all this. Then, with the whistle's final far echo in his ears, he sought more complete shelter.

Entering the big central building of the flat

3

he met with a burst of culinary fragrance that made him slightly dizzy. For sixteen long hours had passed since he last tasted food and hunger was a demanding, gnawing torment in him. However, before he could think of buying a meal, another problem had to be settled.

Of a clerk behind a register desk of sorts, Waddell asked his question. What was the stage fare to Midas Hill? The answer he got further tightened the lines about his mouth. Hunger, apparently, was something he had to live with for a while.

Next stage out, he further learned, would be around daylight next morning, so be faced another uncomfortable realization. A chair would have to serve as his couch this night. He found one in a far corner of the barroom and settled into it.

Some customers were at the bar. Several miners, a mule skinner or two, a couple of hostlers with the reek of the corral on them. Apart from the others stood the gambler who had left the train with Waddell.

In another part of the building a supper gong jangled. Came a quick downing of drinks and hurried departure. Soon only the bartender, the gambler and Waddell were left. Slouched low in his chair, Waddell had pulled his hat low over his eyes. He was weaker than be thought, with something almost like stupor creeping up on him. He did not notice the gambler beside him until the fellow spoke.

'Call it none of my business if you want, friend, but I'm remembering you and I rode the rattler together from Spanish Junction. It was a long, slow drag and I'm hungry. You must be, too. What say we go eat?'

Waddell stirred, pushed back his hat and looked up. His first reaction was one of suspicious resentment, which he came close to voicing. Then, noting a certain honesty in the gambler's regard, his answer was merely gruff.

'For me the food would have to be free. I got just enough money to buy stage fare to Midas Hill.'

'Then I'll stake you to supper,' the gambler said. 'I hate to eat alone.'

Dark pride rose in Waddell. He shook his head.

'Sponge on a stranger? No thanks!'

The gambler showed a flash of his white-toothed smile.

'There's an angle easy taken care of. Me, I'm MacSwain. Once Jonathan to fond parents, but better known in the profession as Ace. Now I'm no longer a stranger. So, come along.'

Waddell considered him narrowly. 'Mister, I don't understand this. What's it to you if I'm hungry? You never laid eyes on me before today.'

Ace MacSwain shrugged. 'Quite true. Yet I happen to have a fair knack for reading people; in my profession you develop that, else

5

you don't last very long. Right now I see you as a man not completely well. So—what the hell! I wouldn't enjoy my own meal if I knew you were going hungry for the lack of a dollar or two.'

Some of the hard edge of suspicion faded from Waddell's glance.

'You're the first gambler I ever met up with who gave a thin damn about anyone else. All those I've known were a pretty cold blooded lot.'

'Which I can be myself, when I've a well-heeled sucker at my table,' MacSwain declared cheerfully. 'On the other hand I occasionally respond to a decent human impulse. Do we eat?'

Mere thought of hot food started the juices running in Waddell's mouth and deepened the gnawing emptiness in him until it became acute pain.

'You tempt me, man—you tempt me!' he admitted huskily. 'You're hitting me where my resistance is mighty low.' In abrupt decision he hoisted to his feet, a trifle unsteady. He held out his hand. 'Waddell, here—Chris Waddell.'

The mess hall was a long narrow room opening into a kitchen at the far end. It held three oil-cloth covered tables with benches on either side. A couple of tired looking women brought platters of elk steaks and boiled potatoes and bread, and steaming coffee in heavy, white china pitchers.

At first, Chris Waddell had attention for nothing but the food, which, while coarse and plain, was hot and nourishing, and to him, enormously good. It warmed him and renewed his strength.

A late arrival took seat beside him. A burly man with a broad, weathered face, short, thick arms and calloused fists. His shirt was of heavy gray wool and gave off the mixed effluvia of tobacco, harness soap and mule sweat. He had sharp blue eyes under shaggy brows and as he dug into his food his glance flashed about with friendly interest. Across the table a man spoke.

'You making another night haul, Barney?'

The late arrival nodded. 'Just finished loading my wagons.'

The other made pessimistic observation. 'Some fine evening you and your mules and wagons will end up in the deepest hole in Granite Canyon, instead of at Midas Hill. Jerklining that canyon road in the dark is playing with suicide.'

'Not with a team like I got,' differed the burly one. 'And I figger it safer to haul that canyon stretch by night than by day. For one thing you hardly ever meet anything coming through—at least no heavy stuff. Most generally you got the road to yourself.'

With the first demanding edge of his hunger taken care of, Chris Waddell straightened and looked around. With single exception, every diner was a man. The exception was the girl

7

who had been on the train. She sat across and down table a little way, conversing easily with a middle-aged man wearing steel rimmed spectacles and the black, elastic halfsleeves of a storekeeper. Her manner was wholly natural and unaffected, and once some remark by her companion sent her off into a little gust of laughter that carried to Waddell like clear music and drew his direct regard.

She seemed to sense his interest, for her head turned and for a few long seconds she met and held his glance fully. Her manner was curious, but entirely impersonal and Waddell saw that here was a thoroughly honest person, serene, confident, sure of herself.

He returned his attention to his food, and the next time he looked up he found that the girl and her companion had finished their meal and left. Beside him, Ace MacSwain leaned back, sighed and lit a cigar, proffering its mate to Waddell, who shook his head.

'Too rich for my blood. Can't afford to renew my taste for such just now. I'll make out with Durham.'

He produced tobacco and papers and built a careful cigarette.

'Don't know how to thank you,' he went on. 'I'm beginning to live again.'

The gambler waved an airy hand. 'Satisfaction is all mine. Now I'm off to see if I can stir up a little game to kill what promises to be a long and empty evening.'

'Me,' said Waddell, 'I think I can find room for one more cup of this coffee.'

Ace MacSwain slapped him on the shoulder and went away.

Waddell, dragging deep on his cigarette, turned presently to the burly teamster beside him, who was still chewing busily.

'A night haul must run a little lonely at times, doesn't it, friend?'

The teamster gave him a quick, solid look, then shrugged.

'You ride the box of a Merivale freighter as long as I have, you get used to being alone. Why d'you mention it?'

'I'd enjoy keeping you company as far as Midas Hill.'

The teamster grunted. 'So that's it! Lookin' for a ride, eh?'

'Yes,' admitted Waddell quietly. 'Yes, I am.'

'Be a stage you can ride in the mornin'.'

'Quite so,' Waddell agreed. 'But for a price.'

'Short of money?'

'Yes.'

'The teamster squared around to face Waddell more fully, and gave him another hard, direct scrutiny.

'You look kinda ga'nted down—like you might have been sick.'

'Let's say I've been a little off my feed.'

'Midas Hill,' the teamster declared with slow emphasis, 'is one rough, tough camp. No place for a sick man.'

'I'm not that bad off,' Waddell said. 'Sorry I bothered you.'

He started to leave, but the teamster caught hold of him and drew him back, growling.

'I didn't say you couldn't ride, did I? Don't usually haul anybody, but every once in a while I make an exception. What's your name?'

'Chris Waddell.'

The teamster considered it. 'Sounds all right. Square and straight-forward. Me, I'm Barney Guilfoyle. My wagons are alongside Jess Blasford's warehouse. See you there in mebbe fifteen, twenty minutes.'

'I'll be waiting,' Waddell told him.

Leaving the mess hall, Waddell killed a little time in the barroom, where Ace MacSwain and three others were already at a poker table. MacSwain was riffling a newly opened pack of cards. It had been Waddell's thought to let the gambler know of his good fortune in locating a free ride to Midas Hill, but now decided against bothering him, and so presently passed on into the outer night.

Thick dusk held the land and the air carried the biting breath of the mountains with all its wild, free flavors. Barney Guilfoyle's outfit stood where he said it would be. Lead wagon and back action bulked high and ponderous under the early stars and the long string of mules, with a roustabout keeping an eye on them, were restless in the deepening chill, and their shifting and stamping kept trace and chain in a constant clank and rattle.

The warehouse was dark, but in the store next door, hanging lamps flung down their cones of yellow light. Peering through a dusty window, Chris Waddell saw the girl of the train and supper table and her storekeeper companion in spirited discussion with Barney Guilfoyle. On the counter beside them were the girl's two items of luggage, the canvas sided gripsack and the rattan valise. Presently Barney tossed his hands in a gesture of surrender and picked up the valise. The girl lifted down the canvas gripsack and followed him out into the night.

The teamster was mumbling and growling.

'Talk about a mule being stubborn. Hell awheelin'! Ain't nothin' can match a contrary female for stubborn when she gets her mind set. I'm telling you, Norma Vespasian, long before we drag into Midas Hill around daylight tomorrow, you'll be that tired and cold and beat out, you'll wish you'd never heard of me and my freight outfit.'

The girl gave laughing answer.

'Oh, Barney—don't be such an old bear! I promise I'll not complain or fall asleep. Besides, you're really doing the favor for Jack Millerson, not for me.'

'No matter,' argued the teamster, 'I still don't like it. It ain't just the money—it's you, too. Supposin' this is the night I happen to go off the canyon road and you get your pretty neck broke—what'll your Pa have to say about that?'

'You're not going off the canyon road and you know it,' retorted the girl. 'So hush your mumbling and grumbling.'

They came along the warehouse platform, thus amicably bickering. Chris Waddell stepped from the shadows.

'On hand as promised, friend.'

'Huh!' exclaimed Barney, coming to a startled halt. 'Oh, yeah—it's you. Doggoned if I didn't near forget all about you, what with the way I been argued at and pushed around by Jess Blasford and this here young woman. Norma, this feller is ridin' with us. What was that name, now? Waddell, was it? That's right—Chris Waddell. And this here is Norma Vespasian. She's ridin', too.'

The girl stood very still and when she finally spoke her words were low and wary.

'I didn't know anyone else was riding with you, Barney. You—you should have told me.'

'Didn't have a chance,' Barney defended. 'You and Jess Blasford had me talked to a standstill. No good reason why Waddell shouldn't come along, is there?'

She was still hesitant. 'He's a—a stranger. You don't know anything about him.'

'I know I ate supper with him. He asked me fair and civil about a ride, because stage travel costs money and right now he ain't got much of that. I said he could.'

12

Waddell watched her carefully. She was a slim, straight figure in the deepening dark, judging and weighing him with an intent scrutiny.

'I came in on the same train you did, Ma'am,' he said. 'I need this ride.'

'And you got it,' affirmed Barney Guilfoyle heartily. 'If you're about to worry, Norma, then you'd best stay over and take the stage in the morning.'

'Indeed I'll not!' The answer was spirited. 'I'm going with you.'

'Then quit your fussin' and get aboard. I want to get started.'

The box of the big freight wagon loomed high and the girl considered the climb a little doubtfully.

'Let me help,' Waddell said.

He reached to take the canvas gripsack from her and for a moment she clung to it, resisting him. Reluctantly she let him have it. The weight of it surprised him. With his free hand at her elbow he steadied her to the top of the front wheel, from where she scrambled the rest of the way unaided. He lifted gripsack and valise to her, then swung up beside her.

Barney Guilfoyle made final check of team and wagons, dismissed the roustabout and climbed to his place on the box. He twitched the jerkline and spoke gruff command.

'Hu-up! Hu-up!'

The mules stirred, leaning into their collars,

13

tightening trace and chain. The bells on the hame yokes of the leaders chimed musically and the wagons creaked into movement, swinging through a wide half-circle into a road which thrust straight at a barrier of timber. Behind, the several lights of Decker's Flat winked briefly. Then the timber closed in and there was no light of any kind, nothing but a funnel of blackness, full of chill and the raw scent of resin.

Within a mile they broke into the clear again, the road pitching sharply up the flank of a ridge. Here the mules had to really lean to it and the hard placing of their hoofs struck up echoes from the rocky roadbed and the bells of the leaders sang a measured cadence.

At the crest the road leveled somewhat and Barney Guilfoyle gave the team a breather. The wagons stood high and gaunt against the brittle stars and night's growing chill bit keenly. From under the heavy tarpaulin sheltering his load, Barney dragged a muchly worn old buffalo coat and donned it. He also brought out several blankets.

'Wrap up in these,' he told the girl and Waddell. 'Long night ahead and a damn cold one before daylight shows.'

They went on, past upthrust humps of granite outcrop and an occasional clump of conifers. Overhead the star glitter was one limitless sweep and all the drifting airs which struck in from here and there, told of primitive

14

space beyond all measure. Riding this high wagon box, Chris Waddell had the feeling of being almost apart from the earth.

In time they left the ridge crest, the wagons tipping down through a short slant where Barney Guilfoyle leaned hard on his brake strap and iron-shod wheels scraped and squealed.

Abruptly they were between narrowing walls looming blackly on either hand. Lifting from far, inky depths came the wet breath and booming rumble of violent water. Here, between these cold walls the night turned stygian and the star-glitter became a fading reflection which gave down no reaching light.

Beside him, Chris Waddell felt the girl stir uneasily, which brought a chuckle from Barney Guilfoyle.

'Remember, young lady,' chided the teamster, 'you promised not to get scared.'

'I—I'm n-not scared,' she refuted, somewhat breathlessly. 'Only—are you sure we're on the road, Barney?'

Barney's chuckle became a rumbling laugh. 'Girl—if we weren't, then by this time we'd be plumb to hell an' done down yonder in the river.'

'How—how on earth can you see in this dark? I can't make out a thing.'

'Me neither—not much,' admitted Barney candidly. 'But the mules can. The leaders are like a pair of cats, and the pointers know

15

enough to jump the chain on the turns of their own accord. The wheelers are rock steady and even the swing are plenty smart. And when you got a smart mule, then you got of the smartest critters there is on this earth. All my life I been workin' with them, and this is the best string I ever got together. Don't worry—they'll take us through safe.'

The girl's laugh was small, slightly shaky.

'Always before, to me a mule was just—well, a mule. From now on I'll always see them as something special.'

Barney chuckled again and spoke past her to Waddell.

'Still with us, friend?'

'Still here,' Waddell answered. 'And full of admiration for smart mules.'

'Know how you feel,' Barney said. 'Like you was ridin' on the edge of nothin. It ain't so bad as it seems. There's places along here where two outfits can pass, providin' the mules and the skinners know their business.'

While speaking, Barney had been fumbling with pipe and tobacco pouch. Now he scraped a sulphur match alight, nursed it in cupped hands to a full glow and ran it back and forth across the bowl of his pipe, puffing vigorously. The match flare made a tiny bomb of light in the night's immensity and for a moment Barney's weathered features stood out in ruddy relief. Then the match flickered out and the dark seemed deeper than ever. However, the whiff of tobacco smoke was a drifting comfort.

'That makes the world solid again,' murmured the girl.

Chris Waddell glanced down at her. She was just a blanket shrouded shadow beside him.

'Yes,' he agreed, 'it does.'

After that first sharp downward pitch, the canyon road with its torturous windings became a steadily ascending grade. For every foot of this the mules had to toil mightily and the pace of the wagons became a ponderous crawl and the hours were eaten up by the long, slow miles.

Every so often Barney Guilfoyle drew to a halt, set his brake and gave his team a rest. At such times the breath of the canyon seemed to close in like an invisible blanket, dank and cold, and above the panting and blowing of the mules the rumble of that far down river was a hoarse and hungry voice.

Sometime past midnight the black walls fell behind and the late starlight thinly silvered the way along a benchland, which, after the canyon road, seemed almost level. Here Barney Guilfoyle pulled to a halt in a small clearing backed with a fringe of timber.

'Coffee for us, grain for the team,' he announced.

Norma Vespasian straightened with a weary sigh.

'I do believe I've slept sitting up. Where are

17

we, Barney?'

'Grizzly Spring. Now if somebody would stir up a fire while I grain the team—.'

'Right away,' Waddell said briefly.

He slid from the wagon box, driving his heels hard against the earth to ease the stiffness the miles had settled upon him. Barely had he done this than the mules, though certainly weary, turned restless. Some of them blew softly. Not missing these signs, Barney Guilfoyle called abruptly.

'You out there—who is it?'

There was no immediate answer, just the stir of approaching movement. After which a voice rang harshly.

'Never mind who I am, Guilfoyle. Suppose you tell me—who's that riding with you?'

'None of your damn business!' was Barney's pungent retort.

A gunlock clicked. 'Play it smart, you damned old fool! Somebody is up on that wagon box with you. Who is it?'

Further defiance formed on Barney's lips, but before he could speak it, the girl beside him answered.

'It's Norma Vespasian. And I want to know by what right you—?'

'Fine—fine!' cut in the voice from the dark. 'I had a hunch it might be that way. Now I'll just take the specie you're bringing in to Millerson. Let's have it!'

'Don't know what you're talkin' about,'

Barney growled. 'I don't haul money for Jack Millerson—I just haul supplies.'

'This trip you're hauling both,' came the mocking reply. 'That girl works for Millerson and she wouldn't be making a night ride on a freight wagon just for the hell of it. Let's have the specie before somebody gets hurt!'

Crouched by the front wheel of the lead wagon, and sheltered in its ponderous shadow, Chris Waddell realized he had left the wagon box before being seen, and so his presence was not guessed by the holdup. He slid his hand inside his jumper around to the left side and his fingers closed on the butt of the revolver tucked there. Several times over the past couple of months, as his need for ready money became more pressing, he had played with the thought of selling the weapon. Always some instinct had persuaded against this. For which he was now duly thankful.

He had the holdup located. The fellow was out there some twenty yards, a faint blur against the darker background of the timber. Waddell weighed the chances. Not for himself, nor for Barney Guilfoyle. But for the girl sitting beside Barney. A wild shot in the dark could be no respecter of persons.

Even as he hesitated the issue was settled for him. From the shadowy holdup figure came a curse and a final savage order.

'God damn it, Guilfoyle—if you want to live, let's have that specie! I'm not telling you again.'

Waddell dropped to one knee.

'Mister,' he called, 'you didn't count right!'

Came a startled blurt of surprise. A gun spiked flame and pounded report. Close by Waddell's shoulder a bullet gouged splinters from a hickory wheel spoke and thudded into the wagon bed beyond. Waddell drove two shots in return. Came a muffled cry, a floundering, then the clumping pound of uneven running. Waddell lunged in pursuit.

Over against the timber a horse snorted, then exploded into a gallop, scudding out into the road and away. Waddell threw a third shot, but it was pure and wasted, which he realized as he let it go. From across the dark, Barney Guilfoyle called.

'Waddell—Chris Waddell!'

'Here—and all right,' Waddell answered. He headed back to the wagons. 'Whoever it was, he's pulled out, some the worse for wear, I think.'

'But he took a shot at you.'

'And knocked splinters out of a wheel spoke.'

'Just so he didn't hit you,' Barney growled, climbing down.

From a rack on the side of the back-action, Barney produced a lantern, which he lit, then brought out a small grub box and handed it to Waddell.

'Spring's yonder,' he said, pointing.

With dry duff and dead branches gathered at the edge of the timber under the thin starlight, Waddell soon had a blaze tapering up. The grub box held some coffee, a blackened pot and some tin cups. He filled the pot at the spring and brought it to the fire, where Norma Vespasian now stood, sober and still. She reached for the dripping pot.

'Let me.'

By the wagons, Barney Guilfoyle was swinging his lantern and measuring grain into a row of leather nosebags. Waddell went to help him and presently the mules were feeding hungrily. Now Barney came abruptly around.

'You handled that damn well, friend. Didn't know you had a gun on you. Lucky for Norma and me that you did. Lucky for Jack Millerson, too.'

'How's that?' Waddell asked.

Barney shrugged.

'What d'you think is in that canvas gripsack Norma's been so careful about? Just mebbe five thousand dollars in gold specie, that's all. It's like this. A lot of miners work the back gulches and creeks of the hills and most of them trade in their dust at Jack Millerson's store in Midas Hill. Jack, he turns the dust over to the bank at Spanish Junction and takes specie in return. Most generally he makes the trip to Spanish Junction himself. This time, Norma did.'

They headed for the fire. Waddell's boot

21

struck something that gave off a metallic clink. He paused.

'Let's have a little of that light, Barney.'

Barney lowered his lantern and Waddell, exclaiming his satisfaction, lifted a Colt revolver out of the dirt.

'I figured I winged him!'

They examined the weapon. 'Ever see it before?' Waddell asked.

Barney shook his head. 'Just another six-shooter to me. Plenty of such in these parts.'

Waddell tucked it from sight, next to his own. 'Maybe I'll have the chance to return it.'

Barney gave him a quick look. 'What do you figger on doing in Midas Hill, friend? What kind of job?'

Waddell considered a moment, then tipped a shoulder. 'Tell you better after I get there.'

They went on to the fire. Norma Vespasian crouched beside it, welcoming its frugal heat. The coffee pot was simmering. Barney Guilfoyle had a look at the stars.

'We'll hit camp just about daylight.'

Waddell settled back on his heels and twisted up a cigarette. Guardedly, Norma Vespasian observed him. The firelight, touching his features, emphasized their hard-angled gauntness, making them stern and faintly hawkish. She filled a cup from the steaming pot and handed it to him. He thanked her with a grave nod.

A slow wind, heavy with cold, seeped down

from the country's higher reaches.

CHAPTER TWO

Chris Waddell's first glimpse of his destination was through early dawn's chill mists. He saw a cluster of buildings strung along a central street which followed the quarter mile length of a narrow basin that bored into the flank of the mountain. Midway of this a lateral street struck off to the south, following the windings of a shallow gulch, where too, buildings clung raggedly.

At the basin's far eastern end, mine structures and the skeleton outlines of shaft hoists loomed, and the brown and gray and ocher scatter of tailing dumps scarred the swift rising slope. A stamp mill beat out a steady, growling rumble, but aside from this evidence of activity the world seemed held by an early morning sluggishness. Few people showed on the street and the camp's chimneys were just beginning to give off wood smoke which hovered and flattened and spiced the morning air with an acrid pungence.

Such was the mining camp of Midas Hill, raw and wild and by all accounts, fabulously rich.

Barney Guilfoyle brought his freight outfit to a weary halt beside the long platform of a big store and trading post building. He set the brake and cleared a gruff throat.

'Well, young lady—that does it. Was it worth the all night ride?'

Norma Vespasian yawned sleepily, batting her lips gently with the back of her hand.

'It was,' she answered. 'We got here safely, didn't we?'

'Thanks to friend Waddell,' Barney admitted grumpily.

'Why, yes—that is so. Thanks to him.' She gave Waddell a direct glance out of tired eyes. 'And I do thank you, greatly.'

Before Waddell could reply, the store's wide door swung back, letting out a man whose bare head showed an upstanding roach of wiry, grizzled hair and whose eyes were keen and shrewd.

'Been waiting for you, Barney,' he said. 'And worrying, just a little.'

'You were worryin'!' Barney Guilfoyle snorted. 'Huh! How about me? Listen to this, Jack Millerson. From now on I'll haul your regular supplies, but damn me if I ever haul anything else. Any dust or money of yours travelin' either way between here and Decker's Flat, goes by stage—not in these wagons of mine. Just ain't worth the wear and tear on a man's nerves.'

Jack Millerson laughed. 'Anybody would think something had happened.'

'They'd be right,' was Barney's blunt retort.

'Something did. Feller tried to hold me up.'

'Hold you up? The devil you say! Where was this?'

'Grizzly Spring. This jingo was waitin' there.'

'You say he only tried to hold you up,' Millerson said quickly. 'Then he didn't get the specie?'

'No, he didn't get it. Only reason he didn't was because this feller here, Chris Waddell, stood him off with a gun. Here's your cussed specie.'

Barney tossed over the canvas gripsack to let it land with a solid thump at Jack Millerson's feet.

Climbing down, Waddell offered a helping hand to Norma Vespasian, which she accepted to come lightly beside him. After which she turned to Millerson.

'It was like Barney said, Jack,' she corroborated. 'Mr. Waddell ran the holdup off.'

The store owner gave Waddell a quick scrutiny. 'You threw a gun on him, eh? Any shots fired?'

'Three or four,' Waddell said quietly. 'Either I winged him or he lost his nerve. He left his gun behind.'

The store owner held out his hand.

'Welcome to Midas Hill. Waddell, is it? Millerson here—Jack Millerson. Seems you saved me a considerable amount of money.

For which, consider done any favor I can offer.'

Waddell shook hands. 'Tell me where I can locate Frank Scorbie and we'll call it square.'

'Frank Scorbie! What do you know about him?'

'Just that he's my friend.'

'So that's it.' A calculating wariness narrowed Jack Millerson's eyes. 'When did you see him last?'

'If it matters—a couple of years ago. Why?'

'You could be disappointed,' Millerson said drily. 'For men can change with the years. He should be somewhere about his office, which is just this side of the first corner you come to. I hope he's reasonably sober, which is more than I could say for him last night.'

The store owner picked up the gripsack of specie and turned to the girl. 'Pot of coffee cooking in my quarters, Norma. Or would you rather go straight home and rest?'

'I'll take the coffee and check over the bank's figures with you, first.'

While speaking, Norma Vespasian watched Chris Waddell, her glance reflecting a shade of the same doubtful wariness that Jack Millerson had exhibited. Gravely, Waddell touched his hat to her, then lifted a hand to Barney.

'Been my pleasure to know you folks. And obliged, Barney, for the ride.'

He tramped away along the street.

Barney Guilfoyle climbed stiffly from the wagon. He stared after Waddell's high, lean figure, lips pursed.

'Friend of Scorbie's, eh? Just when I was coming to like him, too. One thing is sure—he knows his way with a gun. And he carries a pretty tough rind. For he didn't back up an inch from that holdup jigger.'

'Could be just as well he didn't know what was in this gripsack any earlier than now,' Millerson said. 'Else—well—!' The store owner shrugged.

'He knew,' said Barney. 'He knew all about it at Grizzly Spring. Because I told him. Yeah, he knew.'

Norma Vespasian spoke quietly. 'We could be doing the man a great injustice. We're judging before we really know what we judging about.'

The first corner Chris Waddell came to was the junction of the main street and the one which broke away to the south. Boards rudely lettered and nailed to building walls identified the two streets as Summit and Ute. Short of the corner, opening on Summit Street, a door stood ajar, and from somewhere beyond it, though faintly, came the sound of a man's snoring. Waddell considered a moment, then tipped a fatalistic shoulder pushed the door wide and stepped through.

A gust of air, foul with stale tobacco and whiskey fumes, met him. The room had two

27

windows, one on either side of the door. Both had gone long uncleaned and let in the light only reluctantly.

There was a flat topped desk, badly littered, and several chairs. A couple of shelves along one wall held a miscellaneous clutter of gear and a ceiling-to-floor closet filled one corner. On the front wall between one window and the door was a gun rack holding two rifles and a sawed-off shotgun. Centering the rear wall another door opened into a back room, and it was from in there that the sound of snoring came.

Waddell crossed and peered in through that rear door. Here the whiskey fumes were stronger than ever and here was human presence, sprawled on a bunk. Here also, morning's light was so thin and furtive Waddell had to bend close to confirm identification of the man on the bunk.

A battered wash stand against a far wall held a tin water pitcher, a tin basin, a badly scrummed glass and a near empty whiskey bottle. Waddell filled the glass with water, stepped over and tossed the contents in the sleeper's face. This brought abrupt cessation of the snoring, awakened a grunt and a mumbled protest. Waddell refilled the glass and repeated the maneuver.

Exploding some thickly blurted curses, the man on the bunk reared half up then held there, groaning, one hand going to his head.

'Serves you right, Frank,' Waddell said. 'You know better than this.'

The man on the bunk pulled a little higher, blinking owlishly. 'That voice,' he mumbled. 'Somewhere I've heard it before. Who owns it? Who—?'

'Chris Waddell. I've been slow answering your letter, Frank. But it had a time catching up with me.'

The man on the bunk swung his feet to the floor, groaned again and held his head in both hands.

'Chris Waddell! I will be damned! Man, I'd given you up. Great God—what a head!'

'Want some more water?' Waddell asked.

'Not—yet. But if there's any whiskey left in that bottle—?'

'About one good jolt.' Waddell handed him the bottle and Frank Scorbie gulped it empty, then dropped it on the floor. He shuddered, sagged, then began to straighten.

'Better,' he blurted. 'Much better.'

He pushed to his feet and moved unsteadily to the wash stand. He poured the tin basin full of water and sluiced his face and head again and again. Still dripping, he lifted the pitcher and drank from it, thirstily. He put this aside, found a wadded up towel and mopped at his face and head. Finally he turned.

'Guess I'll live, after all. For a time there I wasn't too sure.' He caught hold of Waddell's shoulder. 'Man—let me look at you! For sure, it's Christ Waddell. Sorry you had to find me like this, but what the hell—! A man has to let loose once in a while. And you couldn't have shown up at a better time.'

In the exchange of regard, here in the frugal light, Chris Waddell had his chance to measure this Frank Scorbie against the image of the man he remembered.

Here was the same thick, brown hair and broad, high-boned face. But here also was a betraying edge of weakness in dark eyes not as steady as they had once been. There was definite whiskey bloat in the unshaven cheeks and a lack of firmness that had been in the mouth and chin in older—and quite plainly—better days.

'Either,' Waddell said slowly, 'you've been living too well, Frank—or not well enough. Which is it?'

Scorbie's short laugh was unsteady, noncommittal.

'Maybe a little of both. But let's get out in the office where the air is a little better.'

He led the way into the outer room and sank quickly into a chair. 'Must be getting old, or something. A little whiskey shouldn't leave me this shaky in the legs.'

Waddell pulled up a chair, gave him a direct look.

'You never used to like liquor that well, Frank.'

Scorbie shifted uneasily.

30

'This damned camp! More whiskey than water in it. And you try and be a good fellow . . . But how's it with you, Chris? Where you been and how you been since I saw you last?'

'Been here and there,' Waddell told him briefly. 'When your letter caught up with me, a doctor in Mesa Bluffs had just sewed up a hole in my ribs.'

'The hell! Don't tell me somebody got there ahead of you? That's hard to believe.'

Waddell shrugged.

'He was in an alley and I was a little careless. You know how it is. You can watch a hundred alleys and then forget to watch just one. And that's the finish, unless you happen to be lucky. I was lucky. Just now you said I couldn't have shown up at a better time. What does that mean?'

Scorbie searched a desk drawer, came up with a badge, which he tossed across the desk. 'My night man left me last week. You pin that badge on and the job's yours.'

'Now I could sure use the job,' Waddell admitted. 'Tell me though—why did this other fellow quit.'

Frank Scorbie showed a shadow of uneasy hesitation again.

'He couldn't get along with Geer, and Geer set the Spooner boys after him. They roughed him up, some. He wasn't smart.'

'How do you mean—he wasn't smart?' Waddell got out tobacco and papers and twisted up a cigarette.

'By getting into an argument with Geer.'

'Who in hell is Geer?'

'Hogan Geer? He runs the Gulch. Maybe not exactly runs it, but he speaks for it. And Rufe Belsen was throwing the weight of his badge around a mite too much. I warned him about that, but he wouldn't listen.'

'All you did was warn him? Didn't you back him up?'

Frank Scorbie searched his desk drawer again and brought forth a stale, somewhat frayed cigar. He licked this into the best shape he could and lit it. With the first good drag of smoke he made a grimace of distaste, but kept the cigar between his teeth. He stared past Waddell at a corner of the room.

'No—I didn't back him up. This camp isn't like any you've known, Chris. Here the lines between this and that aren't cut sharp and clear. Here the powers that be want the lid kept on—but not too tight. They figure the Gulch a safety valve, where the miners can blow off steam. Long as they stay in the Gulch and away from this main part of town, most anything goes. Belsen, he was getting too strict. So-o!' Scorbie hunched a shoulder.

Waddell took a deep pull on his cigarette, let the smoke dribble from his lips.

'These Spooner boys you mention—who are they?'

'Friends of Geer. Elvie, Lee and Buff. They

32

sort of do errands for him.'

'Such as working over a night marshal for doing his job?' drawled Waddell in open sarcasm. 'Frank, right or wrong you should have backed up your man. I'd expect you to do as much for me. Unless you're ready to, I don't know as I'm too interested in pinning on this badge.'

Scorbie made an impatient gesture.

'I know—proud! Belsen was proud, too. Well, let me tell you something, friend Chris— there's a time to be proud and a time to be smart. Which is something I've found out since you last saw me. Did you ever stop to think what men like you and me lay on the line every time we pack a badge? Just our lives, our skins—that's all. And for what, besides a few stinking dollars? Thanks, maybe? Don't make me laugh! Hell, man—we're not even looked on as real human beings!'

Scorbie got to his feet, took a turn up and down the office.

'No, not even human beings. We walk the streets and dark alleys. We patrol the dead-falls and the dives and keep the wild ones under control so the solid citizens can sleep safe and sound. Yet we mustn't ear the wild ones down too hard or they might seek other pastures, which could hurt profits. And what would the solid citizens do without their holy profits? If along the way, like near happened to you in Mesa Bluffs, we stop a fatal slug some dark night and die in the dust like a lonely animal, do those good citizens give a damn? Hardly! They just hire another fool to pack the badge. Chris, it's a dog's life and I wonder why we live it.'

'Maybe,' said Waddell slowly, 'because of something you just mentioned. Pride, Frank—pride.'

'Pride!' scoffed Scorbie. 'What's that?'

'You knew—once.'

Scorbie ceased his pacing, stood slumped and brooding. 'Yeah,' he mumbled presently, 'maybe I did.'

He caught a hat off a wall peg and moved to the door. 'Come on. I need coffee—black coffee.'

In the short time Waddell had been indoors, day had advanced rapidly. East, the high, far crest of the Bannocks was alive with ruddy, quickening light and color, and before the touch of this, morning's grayness beat hasty retreat. The camp was astir. Men, most of them miners in the rough earth and rock stained garb of their trade, showed in increasing numbers. Down street, in front of Jack Millerson's place, Barney Guilfoyle's freight wagons were being unloaded. Minus their string of mules, now taken off to a corral somewhere, they loomed huge and ungainly.

Frank Scorbie, about to turn into an eating house under a sign that said simply, 'Frenchy's,' stopped abruptly and laid dark

34

gaze toward the neat building along, one of the street's largest, a two-storied structure which carried a sign of its own. 'The Hill House.' Above a short lift of stairs a galleried porch ran the full length of the place. A man had just crossed this porch to its outer edge and paused there to light a cigar.

A neat, tawny man, with hair straw-pale under a flat-brimmed Stetson. He was clean shaven, and, touched with sunrise color, his sharp featured face shone ruddy across high cheekbones. His thin lips, clamped about his cigar, showed slight upturn at the corners, as though he owned some secret amusement and was faintly smiling. The all-over suggestion of tawniness extended even to his eyes, which were as pale and fixed as those of a hunting cat.

Wondering at Frank Scorbie's reason for stopping, then following the marshal's interest in the tawny one, Chris Waddell now brought his glance back to Scorbie and was startled at what he saw there. Just a flash of feeling, gone almost as quickly as it came. But definitely raw hatred.

Scorbie pushed on into the eating house and took a seat at the counter. Waddell eased in beside him.

'That fellow on the hotel porch?' he murmured. 'Somebody you knew, Frank?'

Evidently knowing well the marshal's early morning habits, the man behind the counter had poured a heavy mug of coffee and shoved it in front of Scorbie even before he was fully settled on his seat, and Scorbie took several deep swallows of this before he answered. Then he spoke without turning his head.

'Price Ringgold. Superintendent of the Crystalline Mine. Order up your breakfast. It's on me.'

Shut off in this manner from further questions, Waddell did as he was told. He ordered, and when his food came, fell to hungrily. Frank Scorbie stayed with black coffee. cradling his cup in both hands, eyes fixed straight ahead. While he ate, Waddell studied his companion with short, quick glances.

Scorbie needed a shave. He needed a good cleaning up. He sensed Waddell's critical appraisal and showed some irritation.

'How about that badge?' he demanded. 'Made up your mind yet?'

'Not quite.' Waddell told him carefully. 'But I got it in my pocket. What are the chances for lodgings in this camp?'

Scorbie shrugged. 'There's the Hill House, next door. Or we could put up another bunk in the back room of the office. And there are a number of boarding houses where most of the miners hang out.'

'If it's to be had, I'd prefer something quieter,' Waddell said.

Scorbie considered a moment. 'Rufe Belsen,

36

he lodged with Mrs. Crowder. Maybe the room he had is still empty.'

'Who's Mrs. Crowder?'

'Widow woman. Lost her husband in a mine cave-in about six months ago. Got a ten-year-old boy to look out for. She's been doing washing and ironing for the Garrisons and some of the other big-wigs up the slope. She had an extra room that she rented to Belsen. He also did some of his eating there.'

'Could be what I want. Where's her house?'

The Crowder cottage was one of a pair that clung to the northern edge of the camp on the first rise of the basin rim. Like the one next to it, it was plain, but sturdily built and comfortable looking. The way to it was through an alley beyond the hotel and across a considerable open interval, which put it well away from the activity and noise of the center of camp. After showing Waddell the place and how to get to it, Frank Scorbie returned to his office.

Mrs. Kate Crowder was a short, wide woman with a round face and tired eyes. She looked Waddell over carefully, then admitted that the room poor Mr. Belsen had used was for rent again. Would fifteen dollars a month be too much? It was what Belsen had paid. Any meals would be extra, of course, but not too much extra. And things would be quiet here, as quiet as any place in the camp. Yes, she'd be glad to show him the room.

37

It was a front corner room, frugally furnished but neat and clean. Waddell gave her a five dollar deposit, with the promise to have the balance of a month's rent for her before the day was out.

'I came in last night with Barney Guilfoyle on his freight outfit,' he explained. 'I didn't get any sleep. Would it be all right if I got some now?'

'Of course,' he was assured. 'Have you had breakfast?'

'Just finished, thanks.'

Mrs. Crowder went to the door, paused there and turned.

'What kind of work do you do, Mr. Waddell? If you don't mind my saying so, you don't look like a miner.'

'I'm not,' he admitted. 'Does that worry you?'

'No-o,' she said slowly. 'Just so you're not one of the godless ones. For this is a godless camp, Mr. Waddell. I was born and raised in a mining camp. I've been around them all my life. They have all been more or less hard and rough, for that is the way of such. But this one is the worst I ever knew. As soon as I am able to I'm leaving it, for it worries me to have my boy, Lorrie, grow up in such a place.'

'With a good mother to guide him I'm sure he'll be all right,' Waddell said.

He chose the words carefully and they brought a faint touch of color to Mrs.

38

Crowder's cheeks and as she closed the door and went away she patted her hair several times and smoothed the apron about her ample hips.

The solid meal he'd had the previous night at Decker's Flat, plus the equally hearty breakfast he'd just got outside of, made a great difference in the way Chris Waddell felt. Even though he'd just been through a sleepless night and was thoroughly physically tired, he was stronger than he'd been at any time since leaving Mesa Bluffs. Give him a week or ten days of this high country air, he mused, along with plenty of good food and sound rest, and he'd be his old self once more.

He stripped to his underwear, stretched out on the bed and pulled a blanket over him. It had been his thought that the minute his head hit the pillow he would be asleep. Now he found this was not to be, for the events and the people he'd encountered during the past twelve or fourteen hours persisted in marching through the channels of his thoughts. Particularly the people.

Such as Ace MacSwain and Barney Guilfoyle and a serene, clear-eyed girl named Norma Vespasian. And someone who had been just a hostile shadow in the vast night, back there at Grizzly Spring, a shadow flinging hard command and then gunfire under the stars, and had afterwards fled the scene, leaving behind a gun as proof that not all the shots sent in return had missed. There had been Jack Millerson, the store owner, whose attitude had changed so swiftly from one of friendly appreciation to wary withdrawal at the mention of Frank Scorbie's name.

Ah, yes—Frank Scorbie. What about him?

What about him . . . ?

Waddell stirred uneasily at the inevitable implications such questioning supplied.

There was, it seemed, a critical point in the life of every man, when his destiny hung in thin balance and fate seemed to rear some kind of psychological barrier to challenge him. If a man fail at this barrier, it meant a quitting, a retreat, and all too often such retreat was all the way into the bottle, in futile attempt to cover up, to blot out.

Was such the case with Frank Scorbie?

There was but one way to find out. That was to take on the chore of night man, to pin on the badge resting in the pocket of his shirt, yonder. After all, carrying the badge was his trade. And he needed the job. For he had debts to pay, some tangible, some intangible. Yes, he'd pin on the badge.

With decision on this point settled, a quietude came over him. In the distance a shaft head whistle shrilled briefly. The rumble of the stamp mill was a solid background of sound, so steady it seemed to lose identity and become a form of silence.

He was asleep, suddenly and soundly.

CHAPTER THREE

It was mid-afternoon when Chris Waddell awoke. He lay for a little time luxuriating in unaccustomed comfort and sense of well-being, making the discovery that when a man's physical self was fairly at ease, then his mind could be that way, too. Presently he yawned, stretched, got up and dressed. There was an old bureau in a corner of the room with a small mirror above it. He had a look at himself, scrubbing his hand across a whisker roughened jaw, and decided that among other things he needed was a razor. He built a cigarette and let himself quietly out of the house.

In sharp contrast to his first view of it, Midas Hill was now a busy camp, with plenty of people, miners predominating, moving up and down Summit Street. Barney Guilfoyle's freight outfit was no longer in front of Jack Millerson's store, the place it had occupied now filled with three smaller rigs, one of which was a shiny buggy with a spirited looking sorrel gelding between the shafts. Here and there a saddle mount dozed at a hitch rail, evidence that this mountain country held men of other callings than that of mining. A couple of heavy ore wagons creaked by and in front of the Hill House a stage was making up and taking on

41

passengers and their luggage.

Waddell crossed the street to Frank Scorbie's office. Entering he was immediately aware of a changed atmosphere. The place had been thoroughly aired, and Scorbie, freshly shaven and shorn and in a clean shirt, sat behind the desk, brooding over a cigar. He looked up at Waddell almost defiantly, as though challenging comment. When none came he leaned back in his chair, relaxing a little, and spoke with some ease.

'Had yourself a sleep, eh? And made up your mind, maybe?'

Waddell nodded.

'You've hired yourself a night man, Frank. Who needs an advance in wages. Because all I own to my name is what you see on me. Except this—and this.'

He pushed back his jumper and laid his own gun on the desk. After which he produced a second weapon and shoved it over to Scorbie.

'That one belonged to a fellow who tried to pull a holdup. Maybe you've seen it before?'

Scorbie picked up the gun, looked it over. 'A holdup, you say? When and where?'

'Last night, at Grizzly Spring. On the ride in with Barney Guilfoyle.'

'You mean you downed the owner of this?'

'No. But winged him, maybe. Anyhow, he left the gun behind.'

Scorbie examined the gun again, shook his head. 'I can't do you any good. Just another six-shooter to me.'

'That's what Barney Guilfoyle said about it,' Waddell admitted. 'Well, put it away somewhere. Now would you happen to have a spare belt and holster around?'

Frank Scorbie got to his feet, unlocked the corner closet and dragged out a tangle of several belts and holsters.

'Help yourself. These are left-overs from when Mike Vespasian held this office.'

'Mike Vespasian!'

'That's right. And a tough old rooster he was. Ran the camp plenty strict and rough. He really took the harness off the boys. Which is why they took the badge off him.'

'For doing his duty, eh?'

'For doing it too damned well. A point you and me got to keep remembering.'

Silent for a moment, Waddell presently said: 'They must want a wide open camp.'

'Pretty wide,' Scorbie agreed shortly. 'You draw a hundred a month, Chris. Here's your advance.'

He counted out five golden double eagles. Waddell pocketed the coins, then searched through the tangle of belts and holsters. Finding what he wanted he strapped it on and tried his gun in it. Then he took the outfit off and hung it and gun on a wall peg.

'Time enough to start wearing that when I go on duty,' he said. He moved to the office door, paused there and turned. 'This former

43

marshal—Mike Vespasian, where is he now?'

'He and another fellow, Cass Leonard, are running cattle in the Alpine Meadows, about twenty miles north of here. He gets to town every once in a while to spend a little time with his daughter.'

'Then he has a daughter?'

'And a damned pretty one,' nodded Scorbie.

'Norma, by name?'

'That's right. How the devil did you know?'

'She rode in on the freight outfit with Barney Guilfoyle and me.'

Scorbie blinked. 'Why would she do that instead of taking the stage?'

'Seems she was bringing in a considerable amount of specie for this Jack Millerson. And figured it was safer to come in with Barney than by stage.'

'Yet somebody knew all about it and tried a holdup?'

'That's about it.' Waddell mused for a moment. 'She struck me as a mighty nice girl.'

'No question. But one who hates this office and everybody connected with it since they took it away from her father. Should she see you with a badge on, she'll look at you like you had just crawled out of a jungle. I know!'

Waddell took a last thin drag at his cigarette and flipped the butt through the open door into the street. He shrugged.

'Hazard of the trade, I guess.'

He tramped along to Millerson's and turned

44

in there. The store had looked large from the outside, but from the inside, even though stacked on shelf and floor with all manner of merchandise and supplies, it seemed even larger. Two clerks, an old man and a young one, and Millerson himself, were bustling about, taking care of customers. Helping them, was Norma Vespasian.

Waddell stood quietly, waiting his turn. Jack Millerson was showing his best manner and attention to a pair of women customers. Both were well dressed and the younger of the two owned a striking, black-haired beauty. Presently, as they turned for the door, Millerson following with his arms full of bundles, they passed by Waddell closely and the younger woman gave him her glance. In it he saw haughty pride and a challenging wilfulness.

Millerson put his bundles in the shiny buggy, helped the woman in, then watched as they made the turn in the street and went away at a spanking trot toward the upper slope of town. Returning to the store, he paused beside Waddell.

'Something for you?'

Waddell named his several wants and Millerson, stepping behind a counter, began laying them out. His manner was impersonal, distant.

'Maybe,' drawled Waddell, 'I should have let that fellow have your damned specie.'

45

Millerson froze even more. 'Told you I was obliged. I'll say it again. Obliged. You find your friend, Frank Scorbie?'

'I found him. And hired on as his night man. Any comment?'

Waddell made the statement deliberately, watching for effect.

Millerson lifted an item from a shelf. When he came around again his face was strictly bland, showing nothing. 'Your business,' he said.

He named the amount of Waddell's purchases. Waddell paid him and pocketed his change. Millerson moved off to wait on another customer. Waddell turned to leave and found Norma Vespasian watching him from a short distance away. Obviously she had heard what had passed between him and Millerson and there was no hint of friendliness in her glance.

Waddell tipped his head slightly. 'I'm the same man who rode that wagon with you last night. I haven't robbed anybody.'

She flushed and turned away without answering.

Returning to his room, Waddell laid his purchases on the bed and went in search of Mrs. Crowder, finding that worthy woman on the back porch of the cottage, up to her elbows in a tub of sudsy clothes. Two long lines of fresh wash stretched across the yard, fluttering in the slanting sunlight of the waning afternoon. The air smelled of steam and soap. Mrs. Crowder dried her hands on her apron, brushed a fold of damp hair back from her eyes and looked at Waddell questioningly.

'Want to pay the rest I owe for my room,' he told her. 'And beg enough hot water for a shave and a wash.'

'Of course,' she said. 'Help yourself to what you want.' She paused, then went on a trifle hesitantly. 'You might like to eat supper with Lorrie and me. It will be about half the price you'd pay in town, and I think, better food.'

'I'm sure of that, Ma'am. What time?'

'Six o'clock.'

'I'll be here.'

Half an hour later he left the house again, clean shaven, fresh washed, and wearing a new shirt under his jumper. As he crossed the interval to Summit Street a rider jogged from the alley by the Hill House; a craggy featured man with graying hair and mustache, and a penetrating glance from under shaggy brows to lay on Chris Waddell in passing. The rider pulled up at a combined shed and small stable in the rear of the cottage next to Mrs. Crowder's home, there to dismount and unsaddle.

Frank Scorbie was still at the office and when Waddell came in, got to his feet and reached for his hat.

'Want to show you around and have you meet a few of the boys.'

Outside the office door, Scorbie paused and pointed angling along Summit Street.

'Yonder's the Palace. Toniest whiskey and poker house in camp. Strictly upper crust, you understand. Where such as Byron A. Garrison—he owns the Crystalline Mine—and Lamar Hume, main stockholder in the Golden Fleece, do their drinking and gambling. Scotty Deale runs the place and he's smart enough to play it strictly for the big boys. Should you look in there during your rounds, walk softly and don't stay long. Sight of a law man seems to annoy them.'

The strong note of sarcasm in Scorbie's remarks pulled Waddell's glance. Here was a bitterness that had not existed in other days, and it made Waddell wonder.

They turned south into Ute Street and immediately moved into an atmosphere that made Chris Waddell swing his shoulders restlessly. For here was 'The Gulch.' Here, beyond an invisible yet definite line, Midas Hill left all manners and morals behind. Here was the camp's tenderloin, predatory, sinful, violent. Here was a territory of human wolves and harpies, of dives and deadfalls.

Here was something Chris Waddell hated, that he had always hated. Just such streets as this he had patrolled many times, and now, even before he had moved fifty yards along it, he hated this one as he had hated all the others. For here were the evils and excesses

48

that preyed on simple, earthy men, that robbed them and cheated them and broke them on the rack of their own human weakness. And far too many of them, in one way or another, it killed . . .

Though night was when streets like this one really came alive, and though afternoon had not yet run completely out, the Gulch already had a voice. It was compounded of a man's violently argumentative cursing beyond the door of one dive and the jangling of a hurdy-gurdy beyond the door of another. Then there was the high, aimless, animal yell of a drunk somewhere further along and the hard, brassy laughter of some lady of the dance halls, carrying down from a sightless, shade-drawn window above the street.

Waddell's narrowed glance measured the Gulch and all that it held, from the grim viewpoint of one who would soon be patrolling it. Lights it would have during the hours of darkness, but they would be mean and furtive, which meant a narrow, crooked street filled with a thousand pockets of blackness and shadow, in any one of which, treachery or death might lie waiting.

Miners off shift moved up and down this Ute Street, turning in and out of the doors of the various deadfalls. In the one of these where the man still cursed in argument, another voice joined in, heavy and hoarse and full of a sudden fury. Came the sound of a blow, the clatter of floundering boots and a miner hurtled from the door, to sprawl in the street. A line of blood curved from a comer of his mouth to his chin, and dripped in the dust.

The doorway behind him was momentarily filled with the squat, powerful bulk of a man in a dirty bar apron. Chris Waddell had his brief look at a swart, sullen face, made brutish by a caved in nose and beady, deep-socketed eyes. Then the owner of these turned back into the rancid shadows of the dive. Above the door of the place hung a single, weather-bleached antler and under it a sign read—The Staghorn.

The miner came up out of the dust, scrubbing at his bloody mouth and chin, weaving a little from the effects of the blow that had so battered his lips. His cloudy glance found Frank Scorbie and marked his badge. He came up to Scorbie with quick, stumbling steps, blurting a thick anger.

'He robbed me—Breed Garvey robbed me! I had one drink and gave him a twenty. He gave me change for a ten. When I tried to argue with him he hit me and threw me out. I tell you he robbed me. What are you going to do about it?'

'Do about it?' Scorbie answered—'What can I do? You claim one thing. Garvey would claim another. One of you would be lying, and I wouldn't know which. If you don't like the way Garvey runs the Staghorn, stay out of it.'

Scorbie moved on, leaving the miner cursing

50

helplessly.

Silent for a few strides, Waddell presently drawled:

'Frank, I think that fellow was telling the truth.'

'Maybe he was,' Scorbie admitted. 'But how you going to prove it? Like I said, it would be just his word against Garvey's.'

'I doubt he'd claim it unless it was so,' persisted Waddell. 'Oldest trick in the book, you know. Short-change a bar customer, then throw him out if he puts up a howl. If that was Breed Garvey who stood in the doorway, from the look I had at him I wouldn't put anything past him.'

Scorbie shrugged. 'Breed's a tough one, no argument there. But for God's sake—these miners are always crying about being cheated or short changed or something of the sort. If that's the way it is, why don't they stay away from the Gulch. Nobody drives them down here.'

'Not the point, Frank—and you know it,' Waddell said evenly. 'I'd never pose as the protector of another man's morals, but I do maintain that even though he may be making a first class damn fool of himself, he still has the right to a fair run for his money. Maybe this Garvey hombre needs to be taught a few facts of life.'

Scorbie stopped abruptly, looked narrowly at Waddell.

'Get rid of that viewpoint, Chris—get rid of it right now! Miners come and go—here today, gone tomorrow. But even such as Breed Garvey is a businessman in his own right, and, one way or another, helps pay your salary and mine. Now here's the Belle Union. Man in here I want you to meet.'

Scorbie put a hand on Waddell's elbow, steered him into a shadowy interior, where was mingled the roily flavors of tobacco smoke, whiskey, and food on the free lunch stand. A few men stood at the bar, drinking and idly conversing. About a corner poker table three others were grouped, doing nothing, just sitting there. Lean, dark men, all three, narrow headed and with a sort of venomous insolence in their every pose and glance.

Frank Scorbie caught the eye of the bartender and jerked a nod toward a rear door of the place. 'Geer?' he said.

The bartender nodded. Scorbie went to the door and knocked. A thin, reedy voice invited entrance. Scorbie went in, drawing Chris Waddell along, then stopping so abruptly, Waddell bumped into him.

A window in perfect location for this precise moment, let in a slanting band of afternoon's waning sunlight to strike squarely across the desk where two men sat. One of the pair was the tawny man who had stood on the porch of the Hill House that morning and whom Frank Scorbie had named as Price Ringgold,

52

Superintendent of the Crystalline Mine.

The other was of less than average size, thin almost to the point of emaciation, with bony, cadaverous features. He had a high, naked dome of a head, on which the skin clung like tight stretched parchment. His mouth was small, tight pursed, and his eyes were as black and cold as those of vulture. He sat hunched forward over the desk, a gnome of a man.

Frank Scorbie said, 'Sorry, Hogan. Didn't know anybody was with you.'

'Now that you're here, it's all right.' The words were so bare they were almost a drone.

'Yes,' agreed the tawny one, 'all right. I was just about to leave.' He got to his feet, touched Frank Scorbie with a glance of thinly veiled contempt, then centered his pale gaze on Waddell. 'Don't believe I know your friend, Scorbie.'

'Chris Waddell,' answered Scorbie, flushing. 'My new night man.'

'So-o-o!' Ringgold murmured. His glance raked Waddell again a trifle more carefully, as though he might be measuring him. Then he shrugged. 'Well, they do come and go.' With that he pushed through the door and was gone.

The little man at the desk hunched a trifle more forward, his cold gaze boring at Waddell. 'You hired him already, Scorbie?'

'Why, yes—I did, Hogan.'

'Should have talked it over with me, first.

He got more sense than Belsen had?'

'I'm certain of it,' Scorbie assured quickly. 'Chris, this is Hogan Geer. You want any questions answered about the Gulch, and I'm not handy, just ask Hogan, here. He'll give you the right word.'

'Just so you understand that, Waddell,' Geer said. 'And you damn well better! I don't stand for any of my people being pushed around.' He stood up, went to the door and sent his reedy call across the barroom beyond. 'Elvie, Lee, Buff—come here!'

He returned to his seat at the desk. Three men tramped in. They were the lean, dark ones who had been sitting at the poker table. While different enough in physical appearance for easy identification, yet family resemblance was strong.

Hogan Geer nodded his bald, bony head at Waddell. 'Scorbie just hired him on as night man. What do you think?'

They surveyed Waddell with a supreme insolence. 'Looks kinda underfed,' one of them said. 'Won't be any chore keeping him in line. Long as Ringgold insists on a front by havin' somebody pack a badge, this one will do as well as any.'

'Elvie,' rapped Hogan Geer, 'there's times when you talk too damn much. That's all!'

The three left. Geer looked at Waddell.

'The Spooner boys. They take care of things for me. You get out of line, they'll take care of you. And next time, Scorbie—you come to me first before you do any hiring.'

There was an account book of some kind on the desk in front of Hogan Geer and he bent over it as though losing himself in the figures. The hint was plain and Frank Scorbie took it. He led the way from the room and from the deadfall, moving swiftly up Ute Street to Summit, there turning into the office. He went straight to the corner closet, unlocked it and brought out a sealed fifth of whiskey. He opened it and took a long, deep drag.

'The usual thing, Frank?' Waddell's words were taut with a banked inner feeling.

'You mean this?' Scorbie gestured with the bottle. Hectic color burned in his cheeks.

'Not necessarily, though it's damn poor stuff to hide behind. I mean what we just went through with that flock of thugs in the Gulch. Is that the regular brand of treatment they hand out to a man with a badge?'

Scorbie dropped into the chair at his desk. 'I told you it was a dog's life. That men like you and me were looked on as not even qualifying for the human race.'

'In this camp—maybe,' said Waddell harshly. 'But not in other places I've been. Could be it's time something was done to change the opinion, here.'

Scorbie did not answer. He seemed not even to have heard. That first big drag of whiskey had really bit bottom. Now he tamped it down with a bigger one.

Chris Waddell considered him partly in anger, partly in disgust. And to some degree with baffled sympathy. Somewhere along the last two years, and for some as yet obscure reason, Frank Scorbie had definitely lost the spark of self-respect that had once made him a man to admire. Now, it appeared, he was trying to drown the memory of those days of better manhood in the depths of a whiskey bottle.

Real cause for such retrogression could only be guessed at. But the obvious contempt in which Scorbie was held, both by sound citizens like Jack Millerson, and by such as Hogan Geer and others of the Gulch, made for deep shame and an even deeper burning anger.

To serve as Scorbie's night man under these conditions was anything but a promising chore. Yet, here beside him was one who had once been a valued friend. To walk away from the man and his problem now, no matter how unsavory it appeared, might be worse than accepting it.

Frank Scorbie took another long drag at the bottle, grimacing and shuddering at the impact of the whiskey's fire. After which he spoke, slowly and thickly, as though to himself rather than to Chris Waddell.

'I can remember when if such as Hogan Geer used the tone on me like—he just did— I'd have twisted his damned buzzard neck. I'd

56

have made him crawl. Instead, with Geer—I crawled . . .'

He sucked at the bottle again, voraciously.

Waddell reached, took the liquor away from him. 'Enough of that, Frank. A big plenty. Next thing you know you'll be seeing lizards on the wall. You better hit the bunk for a while.'

He put the bottle aside, took Scorbie by the arm and hauled him to his feet. Scorbie showed only a weak flash of resistance, then let Waddell steer him into the back room and over to the bunk, where he sagged down, half sitting, half lying. He hiccoughed and mumbled thickly again.

'Wise man once said—the road to hell was greased with—good intentions. Damn wise man, that fellow. Remind me to tell you about it—sometime, Chris. Yeah—remind me—'

He hoisted his legs on to the bunk and flattened out. Waddell stood for a little time, watching him. Scorbie's eyes closed, the piled up effect of the whiskey having its way with him. His first snore followed Waddell out of the room.

The sun was fully down, now, and the world softening with shadow. In the deepening gloom of the outer office, Chris Waddell stood and took stock, pondering the elements of this day and place. In his time he had faced some tough situations, but none quite so unpromising as this. To serve as night man under a marshal who was, to put it baldly, a spineless drunk. Even though it wasn't what Frank Scorbie had once been, it was what he was now.

Common sense whispered at Chris Waddell, telling him to let this thing be, before he was entirely committed. Still and all, should he take the soft way out, what might he leave behind? It could be a stained memory to dog him all his days and leave him a poorer and lesser man in his own opinion.

He thought of the moments and men in the back room of the Belle Union. Of Price Ringgold, the tawny one, with his musing, sneering half-smile, as though all other men were lesser than he, and fools besides. Of Hogan Geer, with his bony, naked, head, his cold, vulture eyes. Of the Spooner boys, with their dark, swaggering insolence. And he thought of the Staghorn, with Breed Garvey, squat and glowering and brutal, filling the doorway.

All these were part of something which Chris Waddell had stood in full opposition to, ever since the day when, as a young cowhand of twenty, he'd been persuaded to take on his first job behind a badge of law. That had been ten years ago. It was a minor job, that first one, sort of third deputy and handy man in a sheriff's office. Politics being politics, and with an election bringing about a change in the office head, the job had lasted but one short year. Yet it had lighted a spark that continued to burn, and from then on Chris Waddell had, in one place or another, carried some sort of badge of law.

Through those ten years he had learned a great deal of men and their ways, and also how much you could give in the way of faithful service and receive so little in return. He learned also that the man who walked behind a star, all too often walked in loneliness. Yet, along that lonely way a hard, bright measure of professional pride could build up which was its own reward. And finally he learned that a man could come to hate the lawless and the predatory and all of similar stripe who moved about the many fringes of brutality and evil and profited thereby.

Grimly he laid out his thoughts and grimly he considered them, while the anger that had begun to flare in him in the back room of the Belle Union now became a settled and dedicated thing.

The badge Frank Scorbie had given him he had carried in his pocket. Now he brought it out and pinned it on. He lifted down his holstered gun from the wall peg and buckled it about his narrow hips. With these two acts, Chris Waddell declared his purpose.

He stepped out into the street, into the long-running, smokey blue shade of an early twilight. Here was day's end. Mrs. Crowder was expecting him for supper. He tramped across street toward the alley leading past the

Hill House.

Someone else, emerging from Millerson's store, was headed for the same place. Norma Vespasian, moving with her free, vigorous stride. Waddell slowed, half wondering, and they met at the alley mouth. She looked at him across a cool distance, saying nothing. But when Waddell dropped in beside her she came around with a swift glare of indignance. Waddell spoke drily.

'You're jumping at conclusions again. It just happens I'm due to eat supper at Mrs. Crowder's, and this is the shortest way I know of to get there.'

Color swept up the soft curve of her cheek. 'Why bother to explain?' she said stiffly.

'Just wanted you to know my real intentions,' he murmured.

Emerging from the alley into the open, she angled quickly away to the cottage next to Mrs. Crowder's place. The man who had ridden in at that other cottage earlier in the day, showed on the low front porch.

Waddell heard the girl's quick, glad cry.

'Father!'

CHAPTER FOUR

On reaching his room, Chris Waddell put his belt and gun on the bed, took off his jumper and tidied himself up a bit. Then he went in to supper and Mrs. Crowder and her son, Lorrie, had their first glimpse of the badge Waddell had elected to carry. There was a small silence before Mrs. Crowder spoke.

'You're—not taking Marshal Scorbie's place?'

Waddell shook his head. 'No,' he explained. 'I'm his new night man.'

'Like Mr. Belsen used to be?'

'That's right.'

'Then you'll want your sleep during the day?'

'Most generally. Will that be all right?'

'Of course. It will be just as it was when Mr. Belsen was with us. Lorrie, this is Mr. Waddell, the gentleman I was telling you about.'

Lorrie Crowder was a wiry, agile lad, with a ten-year-old's lankiness of leg and flank. His face was thin, nut-brown, his eyes blue and quick and intelligent. Now, between bites, he studied Chris Waddell with a speculative solemnity that moved Waddell to a faint smiling.

'What's the verdict, Lorrie?'

The boy's glance dropped and he squirmed in his chair.

'I was—just wonderin'.'

'How wondering?'

For a moment the boy did not answer. Then his head came up and his glance held Waddell's steadily.

'Whether the Spooners were goin' to run you out, same as they done Rufe Belsen?'

Sitting between Waddell and the boy, Mrs. Crowder exclaimed her quick reproof.

'Lorrie! What a thing to say! Beg Mr. Waddell's pardon—immediately!'

Waddell's smile widened. 'No need, Ma'am. Lorries got a right to wonder, it seems. In his place I'd wonder, too.'

'But what does a ten-year-old boy know about such things?'

Lorrie, though abashed, stood his ground.

'I know what the miners say, Ma. That Rufe Belsen was a coward. That he talked big and slapped the drunks around. But when the Spooners took after him he lost his nerve and run. That's what the miners say.'

'And I don't care what the miners say,' Mrs. Crowder asserted determinedly. 'I won't have you repeating such talk. Just remember that Mr. Belsen lived in this house for quite a time and that he always behaved himself. While those Spooners—they're the lowest kind of thugs!'

'Mike—Mister Vespasian, he didn't run,' Lorrie proclaimed vigorously. 'He was plenty salty. He made the Spooners toe the scratch, you bet!'

'Lorrie! That will be all!'

Under his mother's stern admonition the boy subsided and went on with his meal.

As Mrs. Crowder had promised, the food

62

was good, better, Waddell knew, than any he might have found at a public eating house. He paid the cook the supreme compliment of a plate twice filled and twice emptied, and Mrs. Crowder beamed.

Finishing, Waddell built a cigarette and rose to leave. At the door he turned and made quiet remark.

'You can quit wondering about me and the Spooners, Lorrie. I'm not going to run.'

The interval between the Crowder home and Summit Street was full of night's early gloom. Crossing it, Chris Waddell paused for a glance at the Vespasian cottage, marking the yellow lamp glow in the windows. He was held for a brooding moment or two, then, as though impatient with his thoughts, he shook himself and went along.

Summit Street was busy and growing more so with every passing minute. Off shift miners, singly, in pairs or in small groups moved back and forth, the growl and rumble of their voices turning the street vocal as well as active. From door and window, lamplight spilled across the street's pale dust, this yellow glow constantly broken by the shadows of men passing through.

Chris Waddell crossed the street and turned into the dark office. Frank Scorbie, whiskey-drugged, snored steadily in the back room. Waddell went in and spread a blanket over him. Afterward he closed the street door of the office, moved on to the corner and turned into Ute.

Immediately the old, challenging prescience rippled across his nerve ends. Here was that invisible deadline, beyond which the words and acts of men took on a different sound and meaning. Here, even the lights were murky and furtive.

When he had walked this street with Frank Scorbie a few hours earlier, Waddell's survey of it, particularly in detail, had of necessity been sketchy. Only one deadfall, the Belle Union, had they actually entered, and there were a number of such along this street. The Staghorn. The Nugget. The Deuce High and the Last Chance. So ran some of the names.

Waddell noted these as he passed. Also he took mental measure of the buildings in between, and so far as possible in night's shrouding dark, marked the deeper pockets of gloom, the mouths and depths of alleyways and other warrens where danger might prowl and lurk.

This careful survey was product of a lesson he had learned, partly from the teachings of canny older men of the law whom he had served with, and partly from the heavy and bitter hand of experience. For when a man carried the badge in a tough town and if he were to have any even break with all possible danger, then it behooved him to know the physical layout of that town as he knew the back of his good right hand.

In Mesa Bluffs he had misjudged the depth of an alley, and only through the boon of the greatest good fortune was he alive this moment. For the bullet that had scarred his flank bad been but inches away from deadliness. He laid his hand against the newly healed wound and again seemed to hear the round, hollow boom of unexpected report and again know the numbing shock of treacherous lead. He marveled, as he had marveled so many times since, that he had been able to keep his feet and go down the alley and get his man before folding up himself.

His probing fingers told him that though the scar was still tender, it was no longer a demanding, ever-reminding weakness, constantly crowding the forefront of his thoughts.

He went along the west side of Ute Street to the far end of it, then returned along the east side. He made the tour without event and returning to the office, lit the lamp, had another look at the sleeping Scorbie, closed the door of the rear room, and sat up at the desk for a smoke and a rest. For the night hours could be long, and the late, tougher ones still lay ahead.

Musing through the pale haze from his cigarette, he contrasted this night with the previous one at a like hour. Then he had been riding a ponderous, plodding freight outfit, threading the night miles along a jolting, star-lit road through the far and lonely hills. At loose ends, dangerously thin of pocket, gambling on the future with no promise of anything definite ahead of him other than an uncertain and impecunious hardship.

True, in his pocket he carried a letter from a man he had worked for one time in the past. Frank Scorbie. But it was a letter that had been long catching up with him, so it could very well be that Frank Scorbie was not now even in Midas Hill, much less in position to do him any good. Such had been his prospects at this hour, last night.

Now, however, he had a job and money in his pocket. Now he carried the authority of another badge of law. But he still was far from being free of uncertainty. For Frank Scorbie, the man who had hired him, lay in the back room, slugged with drunken sleep. While the street he had just patrolled was plainly a swamp of shady, slimy politics, of which he had so far glimpsed just the surface, and which could make his job a farce and his badge a mockery.

He could, it seemed, carry that badge up and down the street only in the interests of such as Hogan Geer and Breed Garvey and others of that ilk. The law, as he represented it, must face in one direction only. Which was the way Frank Scorbie, by word and even plainer action, had indicated it could be. And

66

that was the way Hogan Geer, the Spooner brothers, and even Price Ringgold, the tawny one, had yet more plainly shown they expected it to be.

Maybe Frank Scorbie's cynical viewpoint was the only smart one. Maybe a man was a fool if he didn't play politics, even if they were shady. Maybe a man was smarter if he just lay back, went through the motions, collected his pay and to hell with everything else. As Scorbie had said, miners moved in and out, here today, gone tomorrow. There were a lot of them, and if they were fools enough to let the sharpers and the tin horns, the dive keepers and the harpies rob them of their hard-earned wages, why should he care? For, no matter what he did or didn't do, he'd earn no lasting thanks.

He owned this camp of Midas Hill nothing. It was booming now, but for how long? These hills and others like them were dotted with the ghosts of towns such as Midas Hill; camps that had lifted their wolf-howl for a little time before sinking back into the mists of a forgotten obscurity.

Cigarette smoked to a stub, Waddell built another, and was about to light it when steps, followed by a knock, sounded at the street. He lifted brief call.

'All right!'

The man who entered was the one who had ridden in at the dwelling next to Mrs.

67

Crowder's, earlier in the afternoon. He announced himself bluntly.

'Vespasian is the name—Mike Vespasian. You're Waddell?'

Waddell nodded. 'What can I do for you?'

The newcomer pulled up a chair, got out a pipe and stoked it carefully. His glance, as it moved about, reflected a searching familiarity with this room. Waddell touched a match to his cigarette, narrowly watching his visitor past the small flame. This regard was presently met with steady directness.

'Understand you did my girl a considerable favor, Waddell. On the ride in, last night. Norma, she'd have felt pretty bad if that specie she was bringing in for Jack Millerson had got away from her. For what you did, I'm thanking you.'

'Glad I was handy,' Waddell acknowledged briefly. 'Didn't amount to much.' More solidly he added, 'In your boots I'd give Millerson a considerable slice of hell. Playing messenger for several thousand dollars in gold specie through rough country is no chore for a girl. Millerson should have known better than let her try it.'

'Won't happen again,' Vespasian assured him. 'Though it wasn't Millerson's fault entirely. Norma's pretty self-reliant and knows her own mind. Almost too well, at times.' A meager grin accompanied this last statement.

Chris Waddell found himself liking this

man. It was easy to understand why Mike Vespasian was no longer marshal of Midas Hill. Too strict, was Frank Scorbie's explanation. The real reason, decided Waddell, was that here was a man too solid to ever compromise his self-respect and personal integrity, or try and stay in favor by mixing in the dirty political noire of Ute Street. Because of the way his own thoughts had been channeling a few moments ago, Waddell found himself squirming a little inside under the direct honesty of this man's glance.

In the back room a gusty snore sounded. Mike Vespasian tipped his head. 'Scorbie?'

Waddell nodded.

Vespasian sucked on his pipe meditatively, then shrugged.

'Too bad. He wasn't that way when he first took over here. You're his night man, of course?'

'That's it.'

Vespasian held Chris Waddell again with that disconcertingly direct glance.

'You make that badge mean what it's supposed to mean, you got a chore ahead of you. A lot of people along Ute Street won't like you.'

'Such as Hogan Geer and Breed Garvey?' Waddell suggested.

'Them—and others. Some you wouldn't likely think.'

'Price Ringgold, maybe?'

69

Vespasian's expression quickened. 'What gave you that idea?'

'He and Geer had their heads together this afternoon in the back room of the Belle Union. Scorbie tells me Ringgold is superintendent of one of the big mines. What would he be doing mixing with such as Geer?'

A sardonic smile pulled at Vespasian's lips. 'You ask Scorbie that?'

'Not directly. But I've been wondering.'

Mike Vespasian ran a freshening match across the bowl of his pipe then tamped the coal down with a calloused finger tip.

'You got cause to wonder. For Price Ringgold, not Hogan Geer, is the real political boss of Ute Street. Oh, he tries to keep the fact from being too apparent, but it still remains a fact. As you will find out—if you're around very long.'

Waddell did not miss the slight pause in Vespasian's final statement. There was an inference in it that brought his curt retort.

'I expect to be around quite a while.'

'If you are,' Mike Vespasian told him flatly, 'it will be because you do one of two things. Either you come up spineless like Scorbie has, or you show Ute Street a brand of toughness it hasn't seen before.'

'Not even the kind you showed? I heard you weren't exactly soft.'

Mike Vespasian got to his feet and moved about the room, a harsh shadow breaking

70

suddenly across his face.

'If I hadn't had my girl Norma to think of, if I'd been a loner, then I'd have really made that damn street sit up and beg. But Norma's welfare and future was an obligation I couldn't shrug off, not in good conscience. So I didn't go as far as I'd have liked to.'

'Even so,' Waddell remarked cynically, 'they took the badge off you because you wouldn't let the boys leap and play all they wanted. Is that it?'

'Yes, they took my badge away. It was just as well, else I might not be alive today. For in spite of everything, I was on the verge of going after that street, all out! Which could have meant a real smoke rolling.' Mike Vespasian paused in his pacing and looked down at Waddell. 'That's what's ahead of you, you know, if you set out to do your job right. And if you do your job right, then Scorbie will fire you. You'll see. They'll make him get rid of you.'

Waddell stubbed out his cigarette. 'Maybe I won't fire, easy.'

Mike Vespasian's look sharpened. 'What do you mean by that?'

Waddell tipped a shoulder. 'Maybe I'll tell them to try and take the badge off me. And see if they can—'

'You stick with that,' declared Vespasian vigorously, 'and you're either the world's greatest fool—or the best man ever to wear

71

the badge in this damn camp.'

Waddell showed a small, bleak smile. 'Probably all of the first. About the rest, we'll have to wait and see.'

The older man spread his hands on the desk, leaned across it. 'You mean you're really set to play it that way—defy the whole damn layout?'

'That's it. Maybe the world's greatest fool, but still—that's it!' Waddell stood up, to face Mike Vespasian levelly. 'It's like this. If all the wearing of a badge meant to me was just a job, then I'd quit right now. I'd go back to punching cattle, where the wear and tear is less. But when I pin on a star, I seem to put on something else, something that carries a high, bright shine. Oh, nobody else can see that shine, maybe. But I can see it. And if I backed away now, the shine would be lost forever and I'd be a pretty poor man, with little use for myself.'

He took a short turn about the room, then paused to face Mike Vespasian again.

'All my life I've hated streets like Ute. Not because of the poor, hard working devils who spend their money there, but because of the shoddy return they get for it. Cheated, robbed, fed rot-gut instead of decent liquor. And when their pockets are empty, thrown out in the street like they were dogs. If that's the whole measure of a man's worth in this world, then it's a damn sorry world. And I'm not ready to subscribe to that, yet. Not if I have to shoot hell out of a flock of such as Hogan Geer, the Spooners and Breed Garvey!'

He stood for a moment, staring straight ahead, his jaw ridged and hard. Abruptly he gave a short, apologetic laugh and swung around.

'Sorry. Didn't mean to be so mouthy. Don't know what made me climb a chair and shout that way. Doesn't make much sense, does it?'

Mike Vespasian moved to the door and paused there, eyeing Waddell gravely.

'It makes all kinds of sense—providing you can make it stick. Even if you do, there'll be few who'll appreciate it. You're facing a thankless job, which I damn well know—having handled it myself. Once more, obliged for the favor you did my Norma. For the rest—it'll be interesting. Yeah, interesting. I wish you luck!'

Chris Waddell watched the door close and considered it for a little time, again telling himself that he liked the man who had just left. After which he blew out the lamp and stepped again into the night.

Summit Street was beginning to close up. Many of the buildings were already dark and, even as he watched, the lights in Millerson's store went out. Brightest glow still reflecting, came from the Hill House and the Palace Saloon. Waddell watched Mike Vespasian's erect, vigorously striding figure pass the corner of the Hill House and turn into the alley there. After which, he himself moved to the corner and turned along Ute.

Here there was no lessening of the night's activity. The voice of Ute Street had taken on a jungle note, a wildness. It was compounded of the clatter of many bootheels moving up and down the slatted board sidewalks, the tinny banging of piano and hurdy-gurdy, the high, hard, brassy laughter of dance hall girls, the rumble of men's voices, full of cursing and a rising roughness as their liquor took hold. Somewhere a drunk was singing, badly off key, and another was lifting shrill, senseless wolf howls at the chilling stars.

Waddell passed men who weaved and staggered as they walked, some silent, some mumbling their muddled drunken thoughts. He passed a miner sitting on the edge of the walk, hunched and sick and miserable. He passed another lying half in, half out of a dark pocket. This one he knelt beside for a moment, to make sure he was suffering from nothing worse than drunken sleep. There was no point in trying to rouse the fellow, someone had already gone through his pockets. Waddell hauled his legs around, rolled him closer to the wall and left him so.

Ute Street! Straightening, Chris Waddell looked along it, hating it. At his right hand was the door of a deadfall. Above the door hung a single bleached antler. The Staghorn. With a

74

hard swing of his shoulders, Waddell turned in here.

The room was heavy with many odors. Of men and their sweat and of the mud and earth stained clothes they toiled and lived in. Of tobacco smoke which streamed and eddied about the lights, part smothering the glow and leaving the further limits of the room in murky shadow. And of the strong, sweet reek of cheap whiskey.

Waddell pushed his way up to a bar that was battered and stained. Across it he faced the brutal, challenging presence of Breed Garvey. The dive owner, after one quick look, wasted no time in making a flat statement.

'Take that damn badge out of here; it's bad for business. Walk the street all you want, but stay out of my place. Scorbie must have told you that?'

'Maybe he forgot,' Waddell answered curtly. 'In any case it wouldn't matter. I come and go where I please. There's a drunk lying up against your wall out front. Somebody has been through his pockets. You know anything about that?'

This brought a flare in eyes as dank and muddy as those of some swamp water denizen. Behind his bar, swathed in grimy apron, sleeves rolled up over hairy, heavy forearms, Breed Garvey made a broad and brutal and dangerous shape.

'You accusing me of something?'

75

'I'm asking you something. Do you know anything about that drunk's pockets being looted?'

Garvey tipped his head, spat on the floor.

'I don't roll drunks. I don't have to.'

'You just short-change them and throw them out if they object, is that it?' Waddell kept his tone level, but there was a cold ring to his words that made them carry. The room quieted as men turned to look and listen.

Breed Garvey slapped two thick, powerful hands palm down on the bar top. The answer that came out of his hair-matted throat seemed to erupt, rather than be spoken, so guttural was it.

'Keep on pushing and I'll throw you out.'

'A chore,' taunted Waddell, 'you could break your face on!'

Watching alertly, he saw the animal rage flare in Garvey, and was set for the move which came, and so swung head and shoulders back and made Garvey's grab for him across the bar fall short. Just as swiftly he came forward again and with a drawn gun which he slashed solidly across Garvey's face.

It was a savage, calculated blow and it piled Breed Garvey up behind his bar like an axed bull.

Came a long moment of dead silence. Then a man said thinly:

'Mister, that was pretty damn rough!'

Waddell's glance sought out the speaker. He

stood at the far end of the bar, hatchet-faced, with rusty hair and a lank, down-curving mustache to frame a narrow mouth and pointed chin. The murky lamplight brought out a hint of pallor under the weather tan on his face. By his clothes he was no miner, rather an itinerant saddle hand of sorts. A blanket lined, canvas coat hung on his shoulders, one sleeve empty. The arm that ordinarily would have filled this was tucked across his chest bandaged and supported in a sling.

'Rough?' Waddell retorted. 'Yes. And meant to be. You—what happened to your arm?' Speaking, he moved in on the man.

Whatever had been in the fellow's mind when he made his first remark, it was plain that he now regretted it, for Waddell was laying the pressure on him and he couldn't stand up to it. He gave ground with a surly evasiveness.

'What's my arm to you?'

'I'm asking you—what happened to it?'

'I busted it. Bronc threw me.'

'Where did this happen? At Grizzly Spring, maybe?'

The fellow's lids crept down and he stared woodenly. 'Never heard of such a place.'

'Sure of that?' Waddell kept the pressure on.

'I said so, didn't I?'

'You could be lying.'

To this came no answer, just that wooden

stare.

'You should,' said Waddell sarcastically, 'learn to sit a saddle better.'

With this he turned, shouldered his way through the crowd and went out.

Moving on along Ute Street, his stride felt freer, more expansive. His mind was cleaned of any last touch of indecision, of all doubt of what his future course would be. Now the statements he had made to Mike Vespasian in the office a short time ago, took on their fullest meaning.

He was fully committed, past the point of possible return. By pistol-whipping Breed Garvey he had taken his stand, delivered his challenge to Ute Street and all that it might hold.

If he had gone a long way out on a high limb, where he would surely have few friends and many enemies, and would be purely alone, at least the air out there would be fine, good air which he could breathe without gagging.

Making the full swing of his round, he paused momentarily in front of the Belle Union, half inclined to seek out Hogan Geer and lay a few facts of life in front of him, too. He held off on this, however, realizing there was no point in trying to push his luck. Also, it was never wise to show all your cards at once.

And again, word of how he had handled Breed Garvey would circulate fast, leaving the next move up to Ute Street. The smart thing now was to lay back and see what that move would be, and so be guided accordingly.

CHAPTER FIVE

Norma Vespasian sang softly to herself while she did up the supper dishes. A thoroughly self-reliant girl, and one quite used to considerable periods of solitary housekeeping, what with her father away tending cattle in the Alpine Meadows so much of the time, yet it was a great comfort and satisfaction to have him home with her again, even if only for a day or two.

Both of them were looking forward to a future when a stout headquarters would be built at the Meadows, after which they would be together steadily, as they had been back when Mike Vespasian patrolled this town of Midas Hill behind a marshal's badge.

Privately, though she had never even hinted as much to him, Norma had known a tremendous relief the day her father turned in his badge. She had been fiercely proud of him and his uncompromising stand for decency and honest law and order, but also she had owned an edge of dread she had never been able to fully lay aside. It was a haunting thing, ever at the back of her mind, and never did the sound of a gunshot echo across the town, or the feverish rush of men signify a fight of some kind going on somewhere, but the dread would tighten her throat and hold her in its agonizing grip until she again saw that straight and well-loved figure come striding safely home across the interval.

But those days were safely behind now, and the old dread was gone and she could sing at her frugal household chores.

At these she was fast and deft, knowing a full feminine contentment in the proprietorship of her own kitchen. Before starting supper, she had had a hot bath and a change into cool, light gingham. She had brushed her hair thoroughly, and now, drawn softly back from her face and held so by a bit of ribbon, it fanned across her shoulders, shining in the lamp glow.

She had put together a good supper for her father and herself and while eating, they had swapped experiences since last together, some three weeks gone. Mike Vespasian had been particularly interested in her trip from Spanish Junction on through the Midas Hill with a gripsack heavy with gold specie.

'Have to see Millerson about that,' he declared grimly. 'It was no chore for a girl and I'll damn well tell him so. Make it plain it mustn't happen again.'

'It won't,' Norma promised. 'But don't scold Mr. Millerson, Dad. It was my fault. I had to go to Spanish Junction on other business for

Mr. Millerson, and to me it seemed silly not to take care of everything on the one trip. Mr. Millerson wasn't too happy over the idea, but I persuaded him. So blame me, not him.'

Mention of the matter led to further discussion of the all-night ride on Barney Guilfoyle's freight outfit, of the holdup attempt at Grizzly Spring and of one Chris Waddell, the tall, quiet stranger who had blocked that attempt with harsh efficiency. And of how that same Chris Waddell was now carrying the night man's badge under Marshal Frank Scorbie.

'Which means,' Norma remarked with some spirit, 'that he'll side in with Ute Street and all it stands for just as Frank Scorbie has done. Crooked men, to handle crooked law!'

'Maybe.' Mike Vespasian had only partially conceded the point. 'So far, from what we surely know about him, he shapes up a pretty good man. I certainly like the way he handled things at Grizzly Spring. I owe him thanks for that, and I'm going to look him up and tell him so.'

Which was where Mike was now, and Norma found herself increasingly impatient for his return.

It piqued her somewhat to find she retained any interest at all in this man, Chris Waddell. No acquaintance could have been more casual or held less meaning. She had sat across the supper table from him at Decker's Flat, and

81

she had ridden beside him on Barney Guilfoyle's freight outfit, neither situation one of direct choice.

She had seen him merely as a tall, gaunt man, frugal of speech, taciturn, and for the most part preoccupied entirely with his own affairs. At Decker's Flat he had shown her a quiet, somewhat brusk courtesy in aiding her to climb to the high seat of Barney's wagon. From then on until Grizzly Spring he had betrayed no more responsiveness to her presence than if she had been a sack of wheat on the seat beside him. But at Grizzly Spring he had emerged from his solitary shell into swift, ruthless, capable action. And now he was night man for Marshal Frank Scorbie.

Norma Vespasian had no use for Frank Scorbie. For one reason because he had replaced her father in office; this despite the fact that she was happy her father no longer patrolled the streets of Midas Hill. Another reason was because she felt Scorbie was hand in glove with the unsavory elements of the town, just a whiskey-sodden tool of Ute Street, making a mockery of the law her father had served so honorably. And, she told herself with some vehemence, if Chris Waddell was content to serve under Frank Scorbie, then he must be of the same makeup.

She had finished with the supper chores and was busy with a bit of sewing when her father returned, bringing into the house with him a breath of the chilling night. He rubbed his hands together against this chill and spoke musingly.

'Yeah, it'll be interesting to watch.'

She questioned him with a glance as well as with words.

'What will, Dad?'

'How this Waddell makes out. Had a little talk with him. If he means what he said—and I think he does—certain people in this damn town are in for the shock of their lives.'

'I'm still guessing,' Norma reminded.

Mike Vespasian hauled up a chair, settled into it. He mouthed the cold bit of his pipe while he considered for a little time. Then he told her what had passed between him and Waddell.

'So that's it,' he ended. 'The man is going to have a try at what I'd like to have done. He's going to defy the whole crooked lot of them.'

'But you did that, Dad. You defied them all.'

'Up to a point—only up to a point. I didn't go all the way, like Waddell says he's ready to go. He can do it, where I couldn't.'

'You couldn't—or wouldn't—because of me. That's it, isn't it?' probed Norma.

'That's it,' Mike Vespasian admitted. He looked at his daughter fondly. 'I had you to think of. But this Chris Waddell, he seems to be a real loner, with nobody to look out for but himself.'

Norma laid aside her sewing, got to her feet and moved restlessly about the room.

'He'll never be able to do it, Dad. If he did that he would be going against Scorbie's orders. Scorbie wouldn't stand for it. He'd fire him.'

Mike Vespasian chuckled softly. 'I mentioned that angle to Waddell. Didn't seem to concern him too much. I sort of gathered the idea he wasn't going to fire easy.'

'You mean he won't pay any attention to Scorbie? He can't do that and get away with it.'

'He can if he's salty enough. Sure, Frank Scorbie pinned the badge on him, so to speak, but taking it off him could stack up to quite a chore if Waddell doesn't see it that way. I doubt Scorbie will be up to it.'

'But he'll still be just one man against every thug, every hoodlum on Ute Street.' Norma persisted. 'He can't possibly win. They'll— they'll kill him if they have to.'

'A chance of that,' Mike Vespasian admitted soberly. 'Yet, it's surprising how much weight a really able man can lay out, when he's in the right. And Waddell will be. There's been plenty of tough camps that have turned plumb peaceful and righteous when some certain man started carrying the badge up and down their streets. It could be that Chris Waddell is just such a man for Midas Hill.'

Norma paused in her restlessness.

'There'll be that Hogan Geer and the Spooners and Breed Garvey and all such against him.'

Mike Vespasian got to his feet, put a fond arm about his daughter's shoulders.

'Whatever comes of it, lass, there's nothing we can do. For that matter, maybe I'm guessing all wrong about Waddell. Maybe what he said to me was just a talking bluff.'

Norma shook her head. 'He isn't that sort.'

Mike Vespasian gave her a teasing squeeze. 'Anyone would think you knew the man thoroughly.'

'I don't know him at all,' Norma said. 'But I'm remembering how he handled things at Grizzly Spring. For the favor he did me—us, there, he deserves our best thoughts and wishes.'

'Of course—of course!' agreed Mike Vespasian with quick heartiness. 'And he has them—all the best of them.'

Chris Waddell finished his final round of Ute Street two hours past midnight. By now the Gulch had lost its vigor, its appetites. The honky-tonks had gone dark and silent and the lights in the dives and deadfalls were winking out. The drunks had slept off the worst of it, roused and gone their way, and as Waddell reached the corner of Summit and Ute, and looked back along the darkening Gulch, the street, so far as he could tell, was empty.

Aside from the incident in the Staghorn,

earlier in the evening, he had come up against no real items of violence. He had halted a couple of incipient quarrels between drunks, in one instance pulling apart two of them who were down in the dust of the street, cursing and clumsily scuffling. When these would have turned their alcoholic truculence on him, he knocked their heads together and sent them on their sobering ways.

No reverberations from the gun-whipping of Breed Garvey had reached him as yet, but, he concluded sardonically, there would be plenty of them in the not too distant future of another day.

Summit Street, like Ute, was now empty, and even darker, the only show of light being a faint glow in the lobby of the Hill House and a fuller gleam from the windows of the Palace. He recalled what Frank Scorbie had said about the latter place, that here was the toniest whiskey and poker house in town, and where they did not care to see a man of the law on the premises. Which fact, in his present mood, decided Waddell. He stepped into the street's dust and crossed over.

Above, the stars hung brittle with cold in a sky that let down a biting breath which sliced through the scanty fabric of Waddell's jumper and laid its chill along his shoulders, reminding him that he'd buy himself a suitable coat off one of Jack Millerson's racks before tomorrow night's tour of duty.

Welcome warmth met him as he stepped into the Palace, warmth and the smell of good cigars along with the steamy breath of hot whiskey punch. Scotty Deale was delivering a tray of such drinks to the four men who sat around a poker table. One of these Waddell saw was the tawny Price Ringgold. Another was Ace MacSwain, the gambler who had staked him to a supper at Decker's Flat. The other two were strangers in Waddell's eyes, but obviously men of account, well dressed and prosperous looking.

Apparently, a poker session had just ended and the four were having a nightcap before leaving. Having delivered the drinks, Scotty Deale now turned to Chris Waddell and, marking Waddell's badge, showed a quick and unconcealed displeasure. As he circled to the back of the bar and faced Waddell across it, Waddell beat him to any words, and curtly.

'If you're about to say the same thing Breed Garvey did, don't bother. This place is a deadfall, the same as all the others. A little cleaner, a little quieter perhaps, but still a deadfall. I'll come and go in it as I please. Right now I'll have a whiskey.'

Speaking, he rang a coin on the bar.

Scotty Deale was a gangling man with a heavy nose and long, pendulous lips. His hair was sandy and thin across a bony bead. For a moment it seemed he was going to refuse to serve Waddell. Then he shrugged and set out bottle and glass. Waddell poured his drink and with it half lifted, turned his head to further observe the poker players.

They had emptied their glasses and were on their feet, moving to leave. The two well dressed, older men were the first to pass Waddell, both eyeing him impersonally before nodding their goodnights to Scotty Deale. Price Ringgold, the tawny one, followed. But as he laid his pale glance on Waddell he paused.

'Off your beat a little, aren't you, Mister?'

Waddell looked him up and down.

'Am I?'

Ringgold's tone sharpened. 'This isn't Ute Street.'

'True,' agreed Waddell drily. 'But, like you, I travel both Ute and Summit.'

Hardness sprang up in Ringgold, flashing through his pale eyes, tightening his cheeks.

'Evidently,' he said thinly, 'Scorbie neglected to set a few rules in front of you.'

Waddell tipped a careless shoulder. 'I make my own rules.' With insolent deliberateness he added, 'One of them is to be my own man, in all places and at all times. You object?'

Price Ringgold lifted slightly on his toes. 'I might. I'll have a talk with Scorbie about this.'

'Do that,' Waddell invited. 'But,' he warned, 'when you do, see that you don't take my name in vain.'

Something little short of pure malevolence

glinted in Ringgold's eyes. But he went on out without further remark.

Ace MacSwain dropped in at the bar alongside of Waddell, a shadow of his slightly cynical, slightly reckless smile in evidence.

'Friend,' he murmured, 'I had no idea it was tiger meat they fed us back at Decker's Flat. You don't care what you say or who you say it to, do you?'

Liking this insouciant fellow, Waddell showed him a brief grin.

'I saw nobody nine feet high on the premises, if that's what you mean. And speaking of Decker's Flat, I'd admire to pay you back in part. How about a drink?'

The gambler shook his head. 'But I will have a cigar.'

Waddell watched him select one from the box Scotty Deale brought forth. 'Have a good game?'

Ace MacSwain nodded, his faint smile working again.

'Very. But you—!' He reached out and tapped Waddell's badge. 'This surprises me, it surely does. Though, maybe it shouldn't. For, come to think of it, you never did have the look of a miner about you. How'd you come in from Decker's Flat? You didn't ride a stage— at least not the one I did.'

'Too rich for my blood, stages. I made it on a freight outfit.'

Waddell downed his drink and put his

change away. He built and lit a cigarette and looked through the first smoke of it at Scotty Deale.

'Wasn't meaning to throw my weight around, understand. But I never did hold with the idea that a man wearing a legitimate badge, on making his rounds, has to bend a knee at any door in this or any other damn town.'

Scotty Deale began cleaning up behind the bar. 'They come and go,' he mumbled. 'Yeah, they come and go.'

Waddell and Ace MacSwain stood for a little time under the paling stars. The gambler still fingered and sniffed at his cigar appreciatively. Sighing, he tucked it into a vest pocket.

'It will taste better after tomorrow's breakfast than now.' He swung his glance up and down street. 'You should be able to call it a day. Town's gone to bed.'

Waddell nodded. He lifted his arms, stretched and yawned.

'Been a long evening.'

'I know how it can be,' Ace MacSwain said. 'It isn't the hours that count so much as it is the pressure. You might not believe it, but for a little time I once walked the night rounds in a pretty rugged camp. And before long, every alley mouth, every pocket of shadow seemed to hold threat of some sort. Plenty of such I investigated, sometimes with a drawn gun.

90

They all came up empty. But always the realization that maybe the next one wouldn't, rode on my shoulder. I decided there must be a more comfortable way to earn a living.'

'Like tonight?' Waddell drawled.

MacSwain laughed softly, 'Like tonight. Very estimable gentlemen, Mr. Byron A. Garrison and Mr. Larmar Hume. But used to having their own way. So they press their luck, which doesn't always pay off in a poker game.'

'And Ringgold—Price Ringgold?' Waddell asked.

The gambler sobered. 'There's a cold one. Very uncomfortable to sit at a table with. Gives you the feeling that he is slicing you to bits in his mind. I liked the way you put him back on his heels. But I'd watch that fellow, were I you.'

'I expect to.' Waddell yawned and stretched again. 'One more little angle to check up on, then me for bed. See you around!'

'Yes,' said Ace MacSwain, turning into the Hill House.

Waddell went back to the office, had another look at Frank Scorbie, spread another blanket over him, then returned to an outside world held all in close darkness. Though the faintest suggestion of gray along the far crest of the Bannocks told of a new dawn beginning to hover out there, waiting to move in and replace this night that was so nearly spent.

Waddell went through the alley past the Hill

91

House and crossed the interval beyond. Both Crowder and Vespasian cottages were dark and silent. On the great slope at the head of the basin, scattered lights winked around shaft heads and in the mill where the tireless stamps beat out their measured rumble.

He let himself quietly into his room and was soon in the blankets. The promise of tomorrow, when viewed realistically, was ominous. But for a few hours at least, here was sanctuary. The tensions of Ute Street drained out of him and he slept.

CHAPTER SIX

The combined wail of several mine whistles, shrilling the noon hour, wakened him. And the drive of hunger, sharpened by the rich flavor of fresh baked bread, drifting in from the rear of the house, hauled him speedily out of bed and into his clothes. He washed up, and as he moved toward the kitchen met the murmur of feminine voices.

Mrs. Crowder, aproned and flushed, was busy between stove and bread board, setting out to cool several hot, crisp loaves fresh from the oven. Sitting at the kitchen table was the younger of the two women he had seen in Millerson's store the previous day. She was sipping at a cup of coffee and now, past the rim of her cup, eyed him with a faintly arrogant interest.

Mrs. Crowder exclaimed. 'Mr. Waddell! I hope our gossiping don't disturb you?'

Waddell shook his head. 'Not at all. But the smell of that bread did. It brought me running.'

Mrs. Crowder beamed. 'You'll have some of it for your breakfast.' She turned to the young woman at the table. 'This is the gentleman I was telling you about, Lucy. Mr. Waddell, this is Miss Lucy Garrison. She came for her laundry and I invited her to have a cup of coffee.'

Lucy Garrison gave Waddell a cool nod.

'How do you do!' She took another sip of coffee, then went on with words as cool as her nod. 'Two reasons persuaded me to accept Mrs. Crowder's invitation. One is that I knew from experience it would be very good coffee. The other is it gave me an excuse to wait around on the chance of meeting you.'

Waddell considered her gravely. 'Interesting,' he murmured. 'That you'd want to meet me. I wonder why?'

'Oh, it's entirely impersonal, I assure you,' she said carelessly. 'Call it morbid curiosity. To see if you were any improvement over that sot, Frank Scorbie.'

'And the decision?'

Her glance wavered under the directness of his regard and a faint flush stole through her olive cheeks.

'It's too early to tell, yet.'

Mrs. Crowder set a steaming cup on the table for Waddell. He pulled up a chair and lost himself briefly in the coffee's goodness.

This girl across from him—he didn't know whether to be irritated or amused. She possessed marked good looks, carrying that fact with a careless assurance verging on arrogance. It was a sort of sultry, wilful beauty, to take much for granted and was, in the final analysis, probably a self-centered, selfish sort. So ran his surmise, his judgment. He put his cup down and made dry remark.

'New experience for me. Like a bug on a pin. Or a monkey in a cage.'

This brought deepening color to her cheeks and put a glint in her dark eyes. She got to her feet and spoke cuttingly.

'I see no improvement so far. Particularly in manners.'

Chris Waddell refused to wither under her glance. 'Spoiled,' he told his coffee cup. 'Spoiled to death.'

Lucy Garrison caught up a bundle of laundry from a nearby chair and marched to the door. To Mrs. Crowder she said, 'I'll pick up the rest tomorrow.' Then she was gone.

Shortly after, Mrs. Crowder, slightly flustered, stopped at Waddell's side and set some dishes in front of him.

'She's really a nice girl.'

'I'm sure of that,' agreed Waddell. 'But spoiled.'

Mrs. Crowder sighed. 'I'm afraid so. Her father's fault. He's given her everything.'

'He'd be—Byron A. Garrison?'

'Yes. Lucy lives with him and her aunt, Mr. Garrison's sister. Lucy comes to see and visit with me quite often. I think she finds an understanding here that she doesn't at home. It must be a rather strange household. Though who am I to say such things.'

Mrs. Crowder bustled back to her stove and the care of a frying pan in which bacon and eggs were sputtering.

Waddell had just finished full and satisfying meal when the kitchen door slammed open and Lorrie Crowder came bursting in. His mother turned in quick reproof.

'Lorrie! Don't knock the house down! I warned you about noise. Suppose Mr. Waddell was still in bed, trying to sleep.'

'But—but he ain't,' Lorrie panted. 'He's plenty awake and—and—!' So bursting with excitement was the lad, he began to stutter. He drew a deep breath and his blue eyes were round and worshipping as he looked at Waddell. 'You really busted him, didn't you, Mister Waddell?'

'Lorrie!' exclaimed Mrs. Crowder again. 'What on earth are you talking about?'

'Breed Garvey!' exulted the boy. 'Mister Waddell really busted him.'

Mrs. Crowder, easily flustered and a little bewildered, raised her hands helplessly as she looked at Waddell.

'This boy of mine—I declare—!'

'It's all right, Mrs. Crowder,' Waddell said. 'Boys are curious as puppies and are always looking and listening. They're bound to hear camp talk. Where did you hear this, son?'

'At Millerson's store, first. Then Jack Millerson had me take some stuff up to the Stockwell boarding house and there were some off-shift miners talkin' about it there, too.'

'Garvey and I had a small argument, all right,' Waddell admitted. He pushed back his chair and reached for his tobacco and papers. Lorrie watched him twist up a smoke.

'I'm sure glad you fixed him, Mister Waddell. He hit me one time.'

Waddell ran his tongue along his cigarette, sealing it. 'So-o? How'd that happen?'

'I was in a hurry about somethin'. I was runnin', and I happened to bump into Garvey. I didn't mean to. I told him I was sorry. But he hit me a lick, anyway.' The boy felt of his thin, brown cheek and his eyes clouded at the memory.

Waddell nodded. 'He's the kind who would take his mean out on a youngster.'

He lit his cigarette and got to his feet. He smiled down at ten-year-old Lorrie and passed a big hand through the lad's hair.

'Promised you I wouldn't run, didn't I?'

He went along to his room, donned jumper and hat, and stepped out in the clear, golden, high country sunlight. A slim figure strode from the alley by the Hill House. She had a basket of groceries over one arm and moved swiftly across the interval.

Chris Waddell touched his hat gravely. 'Miss Vespasian!'

It seemed she might pass without speaking. But abruptly she paused and looked at him with as direct and clear a pair of hazel eyes as he had ever looked into.

'You,' she said, 'are either a brave man or a foolish one. In either case I—I wish you luck.'

She left it that way, hurrying on.

Waddell watched her until she entered her cottage, then moved along, musing over her somewhat ambiguous words. By the time he reached Summit Street he decided he had the answer.

'Obliged for the thought, Norma Vespasian,' he murmured. 'I'll need that luck—a lot of it!'

He crossed to the office. A shaky, haggard-looking Frank Scorbie sat hunched at the desk, and he spoke thickly the moment Waddell stepped through the door.

'You damned fool! Take it off!'

Waddell studied him for a brief moment. 'Meaning—what?'

'You know what I mean. That badge. Take it off!'

97

Waddell shook his bead. 'No—I don't think so.'

Scorbie slammed a fist on the desk. 'I say—yes! I'll make it even plainer. You're fired!'

'No!' said Waddell again. The line of his lips thinned and the gray of his eyes darkened. He spun a chair around, put a foot on it and rested his elbow on his bent knee. He fixed Scorbie with a direct, boring glance.

'What the hell's the matter with you, Frank? What's got into you? I get a letter from you, telling me to look you up, here in Midas Hill. In the letter you said you might have a job for me. Well, I remembered a time when we worked together. That was in River Pass, out on the edge of the Rifle Plains. Cattle country. Tough country. And a tough town, River Pass. Where Frank Scorbie was Marshal. And a good one he was, too. For he walked straight up, ran the law fair for all men, looked every man in the eye and carried his badge with a shine. He took a drink now and then, but I never saw him even close to being past the edge. I was proud to work with that Frank Scorbie.'

Waddell took a big drag at his cigarette and stubbed out the butt. Frank Scorbie, staring across at him with bloodshot eyes started to speak, but Waddell cut him off harshly.

'Shut up! I'm having my say. Yeah, I was proud to work with that Frank Scorbie. So, remembering him as I'd know him, when I got

98

his letter I headed for Midas Hill. Arriving here, and telling some sound people that Frank Scorbie was my friend, I found them backing away from me like I had the plague. I wondered about that until I located Frank Scorbie. Then I understood. For what did I find? I found a frowsy sot, sleeping off a big drunk. I don't like that—not a little. So, when he sobers up and offers me the night man's badge, I hold off a little not at all sure I know this kind of Frank Scorbie, or whether I want to work for him. I finally decide to take a chance and I pin on the badge he offers me. When I did that it was with the intention of making it mean something. That is still my intention. Frank, I'm not going to fire, easy. So don't try it!'

'But you gun-whipped Breed Garvey,' blurted Scorbie. 'Don't you realize what that means?'

'It means,' Waddell retorted, 'that the next time I walk into his deadfall, that damned animal will know his place.'

'But I warned you special about antagonizing men like him—.' Scorbie's words ran off into a floundering uncertainty.

'Sure you did,' agreed Waddell curtly. 'You also let him short-change—rob a miner, and did nothing about it. After that you cringed in front of that buzzard-headed Hogan Geer and his pet thugs, the Spooner brothers. And that fellow, Price Ringgold—he looked at you like

99

he was ready to spit on you. And you took it! But somewhere there was a spark of shame. For you came right back here to this office and set out to lose yourself again in a bottle. You, Frank Scorbie did that. The Frank Scorbie who once walked proud in River Pass and made that town sit up and beg. I can't figure it!'

'Don't try,' mumbled Scorbie.

Under the lash of Chris Waddell's words, Frank Scorbie had slid down in his chair and was staring at the desk top with lowered eyes. Something more than mere whiskey flush colored his puffed, drink-blotched face. The desk in front of him was a mess of spilled tobacco and shreds of torn and crumpled wheat straw paper. Evidently he had made several unsuccessful attempts to build himself a cigarette. Now he tried again, but with no better success than before, his hands being that shaky and uncertain. For he tore two papers before he got a third one creased, and when he tried to sift tobacco into this one, he spilled more Durham on the desk than he did on the paper.

Chris Waddell, watching, brought out his own smoking and spun up a cigarette. He leaned and tucked it between Scorbie's lips, then scratched a match for a light. Frank Scorbie inhaled hungrily, nodding his shamed thanks. Waddell built another smoke for himself and waited silently. He'd had his say.

100

Now it was Scorbie's turn.

'I'm asking you to turn back that badge, Chris,' Scorbie said presently. The words were still thick, but the tone milder, almost beseeching. 'Believe me, it's best all ways. This is no spot for a man like you. I was wrong in ever asking you to come here.'

'Yet you did,' Waddell reminded. 'You must have had a reason.'

'I thought I did,' nodded Scorbie slowly. 'Call it a weak moment on my part. Or another of a long list of weak moments; lately there's been a hell of a lot of such. Anyway, I was remembering the strength that was in you. I figured I needed some of it. Now I know I had no business asking for it. So—forget Midas Hill, Chris. Forget me. Or at least, if you do remember me, make it the Frank Scorbie you knew in River Pass. The advance in wages—you're welcome to it. But you'll have to give me back that badge. That's the way it will have to be, Chris.'

'No!' said Waddell. He took a short turn up and down the office, then came around on Scorbie, full of bleak censure. 'God damn it, Frank—get up off your hands and knees! You don't have to crawl in front of the kind of scum that runs Ute Street. Buck up, man! Lay off the bottle. Sober up and get squared away again. Then you and me, we'll handle this town like we did River Pass.'

Scorbie shook his head. 'You don't

101

understand.'

'That's right,' Waddell rapped. 'I don't. I don't understand how any man who had once been the kind of man you were, could become the kind you are now.'

Scorbie brooded for a moment. Then he slowly pulled erect in his chair and his glance lifted to meet and hold Chris Waddell's intent regard.

'All right,' he said, his tone clearing a little. 'I'll tell you. It was after those River Pass days. Like you say, we'd quieted that town down. Then you got restless and headed out for a look at new country. Pretty soon I did the same. I had a fair stake in my jeans, but it couldn't last forever, so before too long I needed work again. Carrying a badge was the only trade I knew. I heard talk that a town called Keystone needed a marshal, so I went there. It was a rich town, but a mean one, on the edge of some wild hill country that ran about ten bad ones to the square mile by the look of the reward dodgers I met up with.'

Frank Scorbie paused for a drag at his cigarette.

'Yeah,' he went on. 'I never saw so many reward dodgers in one pile before. Apparently they had followed the wanted men that far, but nobody'd been able to serve any of them. Anyhow, I hired on. I needed a night man and when a young fellow named Ruel Donner showed and asked for the job, I hired him, liking his looks.'

Scorbie went silent again, staring into space. His face seemed to sag, his shoulders, too. It was as though he was suddenly very weary.

'I didn't know he was married,' he resumed. 'I didn't know he had a wife and a pair of kids back on a hard-scrabble ranch he was trying to get started. But that was how it was. Two young folks, trying to get a start in a tough world. Her caring for the kids and running the ranch, hauling water, chopping wood, doing a man's work, by God, to help her man. Him holding down a night man's job for me because it was the only work he could get right then that offered some ready cash. Which was what they had to have—some ready money to hold things together until the ranch began to pay off.

'No, I had no idea that Ruel Donner was married. He did a good job of keeping the fact hid, because he was afraid I wouldn't have hired him if I'd known. So his wife told me, after she'd become a widow. He was a good man on the job, Ruel Donner was, a mighty good one. Too good to die the way he did, and so young. But one night he did. One of the wild ones got him—with a sawed-off shotgun at close range.'

Frank Scorbie stiffened again in his chair and slammed a clenched fist on the desk. Through the puffiness of his cheeks a momentary hardness showed and his liquor dulled eyes cleared somewhat before the wash

103

of a great anger.

'I got the mangy bastard who did it. I caught up with him and emptied a gun into him. Which didn't begin to make up for what I went through in telling that young wife what had happened. The worst half hour of my life. After which I went back to town and laid the facts in front of all the fine, fat, secure citizens of Keystone. I asked them to reach down into their pockets and put together enough money to see that Ruel Donner's widow and two fatherless kids got back to her folks, two states away, with enough left over to tide her by for a reasonable time. And what happened?'

Under the drive of memory, Frank Scorbie surged to his feet, spread his hands on the desk and leaned forward, the anger in him rising to speak.

'Do you know how much money I was able to raise? Fifty stinking dollars! Half of that came from one of the poorer men in town. He ran a little livery barn layout. The other half was divided between a Chinaman who ran a hash house, and a stage driver. Not one of the real fat and noble citizens of the town gave a thin dime. I emptied my pockets. All told it was enough to get Mrs. Donner started on her way, but it was nothing to what should have been done. And right then I made up my mind to something!'

'Sure you did,' murmured Chris Waddell, who had been listening carefully. 'And I'll bet I can put my finger on that something. You decided you'd never go out on a limb for any town again. Right?'

'Right!' Scorbie growled. 'I take their money and I go through the motions. But damn me if I'll ever put my life on the line. And I'll never ask anyone else to do it, either. Now you know. You know why I don't care if such as Breed Garvey robs a miner or a hundred of them. Or how Price Ringgold and Hogan Geer run Ute Street. I'll draw my wages and to hell with the rest of it!'

Scorbie dropped back into his chair, all the fire suddenly burned out of him. His face and shoulders sagged again. Watching closely, Chris Waddell shook his head.

'What you see lying trampled on the floor— that's your pride, Frank. And you just can't stand the thought of it!'

'Pride!' burst out Scorbie. 'What good is pride when you're dead, with half your head blown off by a load of buckshot, like it was with Ruel Donner? And for what? For people who don't care, who think more of a few miserable dollars in their pocket than they do of a good man's life. I say again—to hell with them! This way suits me and this is the way it's going to be. I want that badge back, Chris. You and me, we just don't see things the same way any more.'

'No!' said Waddell. 'Frank, you're trying to make a mighty shifty bargain with yourself.

And you can't quite do it. Which is the why of the bottle. Every time you bend a knee to such as Hogan Geer or Price Ringgold, you can't stand the thought of having done it. So you head quick for the bottle to try and blot out the picture. And it's a losing fight, Frank—the kind you can't win. What is pride, you ask? I'll tell you. It's something no man can do without and go on being a man. If he no longer has it, then he's so close to being dead, he might just as well be.'

Scorbie waved a loose arm past his face. 'Don't preach to me. Just give me back that badge and call it even.'

'No!' persisted Waddell gently.

Scorbie's head came up again, as though he would gather the moral and physical power to put his authority across. He couldn't do it. Instead he became querulous.

'But Ringgold—Price Ringgold—he was in here this morning. He told me to—to get rid of you . . .'

Waddell nodded curtly. 'About as I figured. Well, here's something you can pass along to Mister Price Ringgold. If he wants me fired, let him take on the chore himself. The same goes for Hogan Geer—for all of them!'

Frank Scorbie blinked, almost wonderingly. 'You really mean that, don't you?'

'Every damn word!' Waddell turned to the door. 'Like I suggested, try getting up on your feet again, Frank. You'll find the air better.'

He turned out then into Summit Street and tramped along it, feeling the need for activity to wash away some of the disgust that was in him. He passed Millerson's store, recalled his wish for a coat last night, but went on past. He'd stop at the store on his way back up town. But just now he yearned for a change of scenery—any change that would help get the bad taste out of his mouth.

He went along clear to the lower end of Summit and at that far edge of town came upon the freight corrals and yards. And there saw Barney Guilfoyle, sitting on the tongue of his big lead freight wagon, working over a set of harness. As Waddell approached, Barney looked up.

'Ha! Been thinkin' about you. Not quite knowin' how to figger you.'

'Don't try, Barney,' Waddell said. 'You might guess wrong, and I wouldn't want that. Just take me as I am. And let me sit here alongside of you and soak up some sunshine.'

'Help yourself,' grunted Barney. 'Sittin's free. You look considerable better than the first time I saw you. Not so peaked and tight drawn. This and that must be agreein' with you.'

'Some good meals and a little sleep,' shrugged Waddell. 'That does it.'

Barney worked a lump of beeswax up and down a length of heavy black harness thread. 'Yes, sir,' he went on, as though ruminating aloud to himself, 'things hereabouts must

107

agree with you. For any time a man does a good job of knocking down the ears of such as Breed Garvey, then he sure is feelin' frisky.'

Waddell shrugged again. 'Case of have to, Barney. Garvey was all set to lay hands on me and throw me out of his place. And I couldn't allow that, could I?'

Barney chuckled. 'Not any. When I heard of it, then I knew my hunch was right.'

'What hunch was that?'

'That a man had come to town.'

Waddell made no immediate reply. It was good to have a sound one like Barney Guilfoyle beside him and approving of him. It was good to sit quietly in the sun, with the earthy but wholesome odors of the corrals and their four-footed occupants hanging in the still, crisp air. Presently he stirred.

'You know, Barney—if I stay alive long enough, one of these days I'm liable to go back to the first trade I knew, punching cattle.'

'How's that?' Barney asked.

'Oh, I don't know—except that there's something about stock of any kind that's so damned fundamental and sane.'

Barney tipped him a shrewd glance. 'Some sick of humans, maybe?'

'How'd you guess?'

'That badge. Wearin' it, you get to be around Frank Scorbie.'

'It's not exactly Scorbie,' Waddell said carefully. 'There's reason to feel sorry for

108

Frank in some ways. But not for them who've made him what he is.'

Barney shook his head. 'Can't go along with you there,' he said bluntly. 'A man is just what he makes himself, no more—no less. Ain't nobody holding Scorbie down and pourin' that booze into him. Not that I ain't saying he's been mixin' with real good citizens, understand. And speakin' of shady citizens—have a look!'

'I see them.' Waddell's tone thinned out and a quick bleakness narrowed his eyes. 'The Spooner brothers, I believe. I've only seen them once before, but they're the kind you don't forget right away. What, I wonder, would they be wanting at this end of town? Ute Street is their beat.'

'I might make one guess what they'll be wanting,' murmured Barney warmingly. 'You. Because when you gun whipped Breed Garvey last night, you put your heel on the neck of Ute Street. You hurt not only Garvey, but you hurt Hogan Geer, too. And when Hogan Geer gets hurt, he calls on the Spooner boys. My friend, watch yourself!'

CHAPTER SEVEN

They came steadily on, three dark, narrow faced men. They moved with a studied

109

insolence, as though any earth they walked upon was wholly theirs, and that all other men must step aside.

'Yeah,' went on Barney softly, 'the Spooner brothers. Elvie, Lee and Buff. Elvie's the oldest and Buff's the youngest. Most generally, Elvie does the talkin'. Where's your gun?'

'In my room,' Waddell said.

Barney grunted wrathfully. 'Durned careless chump! Serve you right if they beat hell out of you, same as they did the feller a'fore you.'

Barney had an old hickory single-tree balanced across his knees, using it as a base to drive his awl against. Now he slid it clear of the harness tangle and laid it across the wagon tongue, handy to Waddell's reach.

'They jump you, take this to 'em. Bust 'em good!'

Watching the Spooners carefully, Waddell nodded his thinks.

'Obliged, Barney—but I don't think I'll need it. I doubt there's anything more than talk in them right now.'

The Spooners came to a lounging halt. Their gaze was as insolent as their approach. One of them said: 'I guess you didn't hear?'

'Am I,' Waddell drawled, 'supposed to say—hear what?'

A quick flush of anger touched Elvie Spooner's dark face.

'Smart one, eh? Ever hear about another smart one, named Belsen?'

110

'I heard. But I'm not Belsen. You can go tell Hogan Geer that.'

Speaking, Chris Waddell slid his right hand inside his partially buttoned jumper. The move was casual, apparently with no particular purpose or design, but Elvie Spooner marked it and a hard, narrow speculation tightened his face.

'That kind, eh?' he said, the words thin, grudging.

'I don't know just what you mean by that kind,' Waddell retorted. 'But whatever kind I have to be, that's the kind I am.'

He held Elvie's measuring stare with one fully as hard and challenging, and Elvie's eyes shifted and the faintest hint of bluster crept into his next remark.

'You expect to stay in this town, don't pack that badge too damn proud. It don't pay to go around gun-whipping people.'

'I do what I have to do to bring the animals to heel,' returned Waddell evenly.

He lifted his hidden hand a little higher now, and from the pocket of his shirt brought out tobacco and papers. He peeled off a wheat straw paper, creased it, sifted Durham tobacco into it and tapered up a smoke. He lit it and eyed Elvie lazily through the smoke, letting the pressure of silence build up.

For the moment, Elvie Spooner seemed at a loss for further words, and now it was the younger of the three, Buff, who made

111

truculent demand.

'Is talk all there's going to be to this?'

Waddell caught him up, quick and biting as a whiplash, not giving an inch. 'You want more, name it!'

He came to his feet as he spoke, a high, spare figure of a man, his glance and manner stony bleak and unyielding.

Lee Spooner spoke, but meagerly.

'Shut up, Buff! Elvie's doin' the talkin'.'

Buff only partly subsided. 'Talk never settled nothin',' he mumbled. 'I get sick of it.'

Now it was Elvie who turned on him. 'You heard what Lee said. Shut up!'

Chris Waddell observed and listened and a sardonic glint grew in his eyes.

As he came back to Waddell, Elvie Spooner's glance and words were sullen.

'Better remember—you've been told!'

Waddell inclined his head slightly. 'And you,' he murmured.

Which seemed to leave Elvie with nothing more to offer. He swung away and Lee and Buff fell in beside him.

Waddell watched them go, and presently gave a short, mirthless laugh.

'Well, well! The Spooner boys. The terrors of Ute Street.'

'If,' grumbled Barney Guilfoyle, 'you're set to figger them short weight, then you're twice a careless chump. Make no mistake, my friend—at the right time and place, yonder

112

three can be mortal trouble. I thought you didn't have your gun with you?'

'Didn't,' informed Waddell succinctly. 'What makes you think I did?'

'The way you slid your hand inside your jumper, like you had a gun hid under there. Elvie, he sure figgered you did.'

'Elvie,' Waddell said drily, 'would lose his shirt in a poker game. He bluffs too easy.'

'So a bluff got you by this time,' Barney growled. 'You'd be a fool to figger it will next time. I still say, after stirrin' up Ute Street the way you did last night, it's damn careless of you to move around, day or night, without a gun.'

'That's right,' Waddell agreed. 'It is. And I won't make that mistake again. Now let's forget Ute Street for a while and enjoy this fine afternoon.'

Barney had square, calloused hands, his fingers blunt and strong and nimble as they wielded wax and an awl. Presently the harness mending was done, and as Barney put his gear away he complained mildly.

'Man's a plumb idiot who rides herd on a string of mules and a couple of freight wagons. Never no end to the work. If it ain't sloggin' over the road, then it's fixin' harness or greasin' wagons or shoein' mules. Which is what I got to do right now. Two of 'em. My leaders. So's I can pull out for Decker's Flat first thing tomorrow mornin'. Yes, sir—a man ain't got good sense when he makes a skinner of himself.'

'You,' Waddell told him, 'don't fool me a bit, Barney. You're a mule skinner because you just wouldn't be happy doing anything else. Right?'

Meeting Waddell's skeptical glance, Barney grinned. 'I reckon. It's a pretty good life for a feller like me who's got no kin to tie him down. I like bein' on the move and bein' with mules and such critters. And now, if you ain't got anythink better on your mind right now, how about runnin' the forge for me?'

'You got yourself a helper,' Waddell told him briskly.

The forge stood under a small, open sided shed, close to the corrals. It had been in use by another teamster just a short time before and still held a waning glow. Waddell freshened this as Barney came up, leading his two mules. The best part of three hours was used up in the shoeing chore, for Barney worked slowly and with care.

'Lame mule's no better than a dead one,' he said, justifying that care. 'In my time I've seen more than one long haul bogged down because somebody got careless or tried to make a shoein' job a hurry up one. A critter's got just as much right to sound feet as a human has.'

Waddell did not argue the point, for these hours were agreeable ones to him. The clangor of hammer on anvil, the acrid breath of the forge, the not unpleasant sour-sweet stench of scorched hoof rind as Barney pared and fitted then fitted again, these things took him back to earlier days that were a long way away from the Ute Streets of the world. When the chore was done he swung his shoulders restlessly.

'Barney, alongside of a cattleman who trades his saddle for a badge of law, a mule skinner is the smartest man in the world.'

Barney eyed him for a keen moment.

'Law feller I once knew, kept himself in balance by hittin' the saddle on long rides durin' his off hours. Should the idea appeal to you, get hold of Tim Roach. In addition to runnin' the stage line between here and Decker's Flat, he hires out livery rigs and saddle nags. Do you good to ride, mebbe. Lot of interesting country round about these parts.'

Later, through the waning afternoon, Waddell headed back up town and turned into Millerson's store. In a partially glassed cubby at the far end of a long counter, Norma Vespasian leaned over a ledger. Lingering at the door of the cubby, making some remark to her, was the younger of Millerson's two clerks, who now turned and came over to Waddell.

'Something for you?'

Words and manner were studiedly casual, but could not hide a suggestion of furtiveness which Waddell caught and which centered an interest he might not have otherwise known.

And now that he had his full look at the fellow he felt he'd seen him somewhere else not too long ago. He pondered this fact as he made his want known.

'A coat?' monotoned the clerk. 'Over here, please.'

Leading the way to the coat rack, he showed Waddell a pair of narrow shoulders which sloped steeply away from a thin neck that supported a round and small head. By his attitude the fellow seemed to feel he was a dandy, with an air of superior disdain. But his store suit was shiny at the seat and elbows, and his shoes run over at the heels.

Waddell selected a coat of brown canvas, hip length, and lined with gray blanket cloth. Facing the clerk across the counter while paying for his purchase, it came suddenly to him where he had seen this fellow before. Last night, it was. One of the faces in Breed Garvey's deadfall had been this pallid one, with its soft chin and the show of furtiveness about the eyes.

Waddell dropped the coat across his arm and turned to leave, glancing again toward the cubby. Norma Vespasian's head was bent above her work and the light was such as to throw her profile into clear relief. It was a vital face, with lines of character strongly shaped. Yet even more strongly did it reflect a warmth and a womanly sweetness, and Waddell knew a twinge of disappointment when her glance did

116

not come up to meet his own.

On her part, Norma Vespasian was fully aware of Waddell's presence in the store from the moment he entered. Now, as he paused in the doorway before stepping out into the street, she looked quickly after him and marked the rangy bulk of him, silhouetted against the lessening flare of late afternoon sunshine. The clerk, sidling up to the cubby again, spoke softly and smugly.

'He won't last long in this town, that one won't.'

Norma did not answer until Waddell swung through the doorway and disappeared. After which she put her glance on the clerk.

'What makes you think so, Spence? And for goodness sake—don't sidle! It makes me nervous.'

Spence Munger flushed. 'You heard about last night, didn't you?' he demanded.

Norma nodded. 'I heard. And was happy to hear the law had begun to mean something again.'

'Not to mean that much,' Munger said. 'Anytime you buffalo such as Breed Garvey, then you've let yourself in for something. Either you head for other parts while you're able or you make out your will. When Garvey got his senses back last night, he sure was on the kill.'

Norma's glance sharpened slightly. 'How did you happen to be there?'

117

Spence Munger flushed again, and his explanation was somewhat lame. 'When the word got out, I followed the crowd.'

Another customer showed, a miner carrying an empty gunny sack. With unusual alacrity, Spence Munger hurried to wait on him. Before returning to her work, Norma's glance followed Munger for a little time, sober with speculation.

From Millerson's store, Waddell returned to the office and found it empty. Frank Scorbie was nowhere around. Survey of the back room showed that some effort had been made to tidy up, but there was a lingering dismalness here that contrasted strongly with the ease of spirit that had come to him during the hours he had spent with Barney Guilfoyle, so now Waddell left the place and headed for his room.

Out back of the Crowder home sounded the uneven clatter of an axe, and he circled the house to find Mrs. Crowder at the wood pile, working with determination but considerable awkwardness. He laid aside his new coat and went quickly over.

'Let me do that.'

For a moment she seemed reluctant to surrender the axe, but finally did so, sighing tiredly as she stepped back and brushed a hand across her exertion-reddened face.

'Lorrie's off running an errand, or he'd do this for me.'

'Of course he would,' Waddell agreed. 'But

118

right now I'm going to do it.' He showed her a brief smile. 'A chore of woodchopping will do me good.'

She watched him for a little time then retreated to her kitchen, and for the balance of the afternoon, while the sun dipped and finally slid from sight, he swung the axe with a keen enjoyment.

Because it was good to find outlet for the quickening energy stirring in him. Good to feel the lift and slide of sweat oiled muscles, and to find that his side had healed to a point where he was barely conscious of it, even in the face of stout physical labor.

Presently it was Lorrie Crowder who came past the corner of the house, and he sidled over and stood watching Waddell with boyish gravity.

'You'll have to learn how to do this, Lorrie,' Waddell told him. 'You got to be the man of the house, you know.'

The boy nodded. 'I know. I keep telling Ma to leave the wood choppin' for me, but she just won't listen.' He paused, then abruptly added, 'The word's out. They're makin' bets on it.'

Waddell split a chunk of wood cleanly, then leaned on the axe, meeting Lorrie's sober regard.

'What word, son? What kind of bets?'

'That the Spooners are going to get you. That you won't last out the night.'

'Where did you hear this?'

119

'Along the street. Some fellers talkin'. I near braced up to them and told them off.'

Waddell dropped a hand on Lorrie's shoulder. 'Don't you ever get into any argument over me, son. Somebody's always making talk. I'll do all right.'

From the kitchen door came Mrs. Crowder's supper call. Lorrie hurried in to wash. Waddell set the axe into the chopping block and stood for a moment in the deepening dusk, his glance on the high slope where the mine lights were beginning to flicker and where the solid rumble of the stamps laid a weighty overtone across the early night. These things gave purpose to the existence of Midas Hill, were evidences of basic purpose and integrity. But yonder across the darkening room tops, the threat of Ute Street lay in wait.

So now the ease of spirit Chris Waddell had found during the better casual hours of the afternoon began to seep out of him, and by the time he had washed up and taken his place at the supper table, he was again a silent, taciturn man, locked in a solitary remoteness which both Lorrie and his mother fretted about, but respected.

Supper done with, Waddell built and lit a cigarette as he went to his room, there to buckle on his gun and don his new coat before letting himself out into the night again. Here was full dark, and across the interval in a window of the Vespasian home lamplight was a pale yellow glow. Observing this, in his mind's eye he pictured Norma Vespasian as she might look, aproned and competent about her supper and other household chores. Moving toward the alley, he mused soberly at the increasing awareness this girl was occupying in his thoughts.

He tramped the length of the alley and as he emerged into Summit Street, Ace MacSwain's voice reached out from a corner of the Hill House hotel porch.

'Head's up at all times, my friend!'

Waddell swung over there. The gambler was a dark shadow against the hotel rail.

'Any particular reason, Ace?'

The gambler drew deeply on a fragrant perfecto. 'Talk,' he briefly explained. 'Here and there. About your chances for the night.'

'You're the second with that word,' Waddell said, his tone thinning. 'Seems some in this damn town need a lesson. They keep asking for it, they'll get it.'

'Make it cagy,' cautioned MacSwain. 'Don't let them pull you into a bad play.'

'Not if I can help it,' Waddell said. 'Obliged.'

Across the street a light burned in the marshal's office and Waddell went in to find Frank Scorbie at the desk. He was stone sober and reasonably presentable and for a brief moment it seemed to Waddell that he was again glimpsing something of the Scorbie who had once been, and this feeling showed in the quickening heartiness with which he spoke.

'Better, Frank—just a hell of a lot better! Figured you'd straighten out, once you thought it over good. Now you and me, we'll—.'

'No!' The word was harsh and unyielding, as abrupt as a blow. 'Not you and me in anything. I'll take back that badge, now!'

The warmth that had begun to show in Waddell's eyes and face, dried up, bleakness taking its place.

'Thought I'd already made myself clear on that point. If I didn't, I'll try again. You'll get the badge back, Frank, when I get ready to give it to you. I'll let you know when that time comes.'

Again, as earlier in the day, came the clash of will against will, and again it was Scorbie who weakened. Something almost like hate flared briefly in his eyes before his glance faltered and slid away. And again there was a note of querulous bluster in his words.

'You're a fool! You got no idea what you're moving into.'

Waddell offered him a final chance. 'Whatever it is, it would be pretty fine if you walked into it with me, Frank.'

'Hell with you! You get no help from me.'

Waddell stubbed out his cigarette. He did it with a slow deliberateness that suggested he was also extinguishing something else, finally and for all time. When he spoke it was with a chill flatness.

'I don't know what you think you're buying, Frank. But I do know that whatever it is, you're paying a hell of a lot more than it's worth. All right—I get no help from you. I'm glad to know just where I stand, there. Now here is my word to you. So long as you're not going to help, be damn sure you don't get in my way. If you're going to stay out of this, stay way out of it. Understand!'

'And if I don't—?'

'Then you'll get whatever is necessary to put you in your place!'

'You're a fool!' Scorbie accused again, and wildly. 'A stubborn fool! You can't brace this whole camp.'

'I'm not bracing the whole camp,' Waddell retorted curtly. 'Just part of it. The no-good part.'

Again he left the office, knowing anger, disgust and a thin touch of sadness. Thoroughly practical and realistic in many things, yet there was a streak of idealism in him to see a friendship beyond its real worth, perhaps, and to know regret at its loss.

Had it been a new and casual friendship, it would not have mattered so much. But when you had stood shoulder to shoulder with a man, facing a common danger in just and worthwhile cause, then it would seem that some sort of bond must have been established that was strong enough to withstand almost any strain.

This, apparently, was not so, and as Chris Waddell now turned the corner of Summit into Ute Street, there was in him a wickedness of feeling not far from outright cruelty.

Ute Street had begun to growl. All the sounds were there. The harsh cacophony of a deadfall hurdy-gurdy, the high, giggling laughter of a dance hall girl. Somewhere in the distance the animal howl of a miner, early in his cups. At closer hand the growl of men's voices, the clatter of their boot heels along wooden sidewalks as they cruised both sides of the street. And yonder a gambling hall barker, casting the false lure of easy money across the night in a hoarse, almost unintelligible jargon.

All these things, these sounds and sights were there, parts of a picture which had, across the last several years, become familiar and increasingly hateful. But this night there was something else, something invisible, a pressure leaking out of every dark shadow pocket. It was a measuring, a judgment which lay in the glances of men as they passed him.

Last night, Waddell, he thought harshly, you were just another new face behind a badge. Tonight you're a marked man. So they're looking you over, and judging you. And betting you won't last the night . . .

Violence erupted further along the street. Two men spun from a doorway, went off the edge of the slatted board sidewalk in a tangled heap, then came to their feet again, locked in combat. No particular reaching sound came from them, yet it was as though a shout had echoed, for there was a concerted surge of movement from all sides as other men crowded in, ringing the fighters in an avid circle, whirling and shifting as the fighters whirled and shifted.

Waddell moved in on the tangle, bulling his way through the crush with driving shoulders. Men cursed him as he elbowed them aside and one even swung a blow at him, a fist aimed at his head but falling short, bouncing off his shoulder. Waddell flashed the fellow a glance and dropped curt warning.

'I could be seeing you about that, later!' Then he drove on, breaking into the narrow clear beside the fighters.

They had drawn apart momentarily, were gathering themselves for another clash. Both were miners. One a rawboned, freckled Cornishman, a Cousin Jack, and there seemed no real rancor in him, for, though panting with exertion and already stained with sweat and dirt and some blood from a scraped jaw, he was half laughing, as though this was all a familiar game in which he found a wild pleasure.

Not so with his opponent, however, a dark, burly Slav, a Hunkie with hot and hating eyes, whose shirt had been half ripped away,

125

exposing the upper part of a thick, hairy torso. The Hunkie, despite his greater bulk, had so far taken the worst or it, for in addition to a bloody nose, his lips had been battered to a swollen shapelessness and one broad cheekbone split open from impact with the bony, freckled fists of the Cornishman. Crimson slime fanned down the Hunkie's heavy chin and dripped on his furred chest.

Waddell, measuring the damage and seeing it not too excessive, held his place for the time. Experience had taught him that often it were better to let a thing like this find its own finish the first time out, rather than to break it up with no decision reached, and have it renewed with perhaps far more serious results at a time and place he could not control.

There was no telling what these two were battling over. Such raw, elemental spirits fought over many things. The favor of some dance hall girl, perhaps, or the turn of a card, a careless word wrongly taken, a spilled drink, or an even lesser hurt, more fancied than real. In any event, if they got it out of their systems here and now with no great harm done, it would lessen any chance of more trouble later.

The Cornishman scrubbed a forearm across his face, blew on a set of skinned knuckles, laughed deep in his throat and began circling his opponent, ready for further fray. He taunted the Hunkie with word and gesture and the Hunkie charged him like a maddened bull,

126

only to be set back on his heels by a fist crashing into his already sorely battered mouth.

The Hunkie swung his head from side to side and spat blood. Under his black, heavy brows his eyes glinted redly and a feral growl erupted from his throat. He crouched, as though to spring. He pushed a hand under the remnants of his shirt and brought it out filled with the ominous gleam of naked knife steel. Someone in the crowd yelled at the Cornishman.

'Robbie—look out, Robbie! He's set to cut you!'

The Hunkie shuffled forward with little, sliding steps. His crouch, and the way his arms hung, swinging stiffly clear, made of him a squat, bearish figure.

'Look out, Robbie!' came the shouted warning again.

The Cornishman backed away, both hands spread and open before him, as though he would ward off that knife, hold it away from him. There was no careless, wild laughter in him now. What had been, to him at least, a primitive, though brutal game, was no longer such. Now, of a sudden, it was a thing gone deadly.

'No knife, mate—no knife!' panted the Cornishman jerkily. 'The quarrel was never of that account!'

The Hunkie was beyond words or reason.

His forward shuffle speeded up, and the bulk and unwieldiness of the close pressing crowd, even though it now tried to scatter, held the Cornishman from escape. The Hunkie drew his right arm far back, readying a forward swing that would drive the knife deep. And then Chris Waddell had him by the shoulder, spinning him hard around, almost upsetting him.

'The knife!' Waddell rapped. 'Drop it!'

The Hunkie snarled, staring with a sort of blind, unseeing ferocity. He gathered himself to lunge forward. And found the muzzle of Waddell's gun looking him in the eye.

'I said—drop it!' Waddell repeated harshly.

For a stark moment or two he thought he might have to use the gun, as the blind, unreasoning ferocity in the Hunkie's glare and the threat of the knife did not diminish. Then, slowly, recognition of fact seeped into the fellow's consciousness and, while a deadly anger still plainly burned in him, the crimson blankness began to clear from his eyes with the return to at least partial reason. The crouched tension went out of him, the grip on his knife loosened, and the weapon fell into the trampled dust.

'Better!' said Waddell. 'Now go somewhere and cool off!'

The Hunkie did not answer, just stared for a hard moment past Waddell at the Cornishman. Then he turned, plunged through the crowd

128

with a bursting show of strength, and disappeared into the further gloom of the street.

The crowd held on for only a little time, then broke up and went its several ways. Only the Cornishman lingered, watching Waddell retrieve the Hunkie's knife from the dust. The haft of this was of wood, the blade ground from an old file. A homemade weapon, crudely put together. But the blade was long enough and sharp enough to let the life out of a man with a single cutting thrust. The Cornishman eyed it with distaste.

'The bloody bugger was set to do me in. Now that he was. Obliged to you, mate.'

Waddell's reply was blunt.

'Been no one to blame but yourself if he had got to you. For it's plain you're a proud bucko with your fists. And just because you can handle yourself well that way, don't overdo it. Next time I might not be handy to pull him or another like him off your back. I think this street has had enough of you for one night. Clear out!'

The humbled Cornishman did not argue. 'Ay-ay, mate,' he mumbled, turning away.

Moving over to the sidewalk, Waddell thrust the point of the knife between two boards and with a sharp, quick yank, snapped the blade in two and tossed the now useless weapon aside. Straightening, he had his good look along the street, measuring its possible future portent.

At this exact moment it was quiet. Then, somewhere at the far end of the gulch, the echo of a single gunshot rocketed against the wide, uncaring sky.

Chris Waddell headed that way, striding swiftly.

CHAPTER EIGHT

From his post at the darkened corner of the hotel porch, Ace MacSwain smoked his perfecto and observed the activity along Summit Street with a careless, but discerning eye. He watched Chris Waddell's high, square-shouldered shape step through the lighted doorway of the marshal's office, there to remain for a brief time before reappearing and moving past the corner into Ute Street. A flicker of concern rippled across the gambler's face.

'Good luck, my friend!' he murmured.

Each time the door of the Palace Bar winnowed to let out a flutter of yellow light, his survey of the street sharpened. And so it was that presently he saw Byron A. Garrison enter.

A little later it was Lamar Hume who went in. MacSwain smiled briefly. For he knew what these two were seeking. They were seeking him and a chance to recoup their losses of the previous night.

Which thoroughly suited the gambler, though he still held to his place on the hotel porch. The night was young and he was in no hurry. Also, there was someone else he wanted to see at the poker table when the game began.

A full half hour slid by and the perfecto was smoked down to a cold stub and thrown into the street before the Palace door swung to let in Price Ringgold. After that, MacSwain waited no longer, but dropped off the porch and went along to the Palace himself.

Here his manner was casual and seemingly indifferent. He leaned an elbow on the bar, nodded to Scotty Deale and called for a brandy and some cigars. He sipped his drink with a careful relish, for he was a fastidious man, and though shrewd and seasoned at his profession, he possessed, behind the professional facade, a thoroughly flexible, human makeup, along with an almost fanatical concept of personal honor.

Ace MacSwain knew all the tricks of his trade, and when allowed to be, was strictly a 'square' gambler. Though against the greedy and the crooked he could be merciless. From those who could afford it he would win whatever fortune and his own shrewd, but square ability with the cards might bring. From one whose pocket book did not measure up to his ineptness at the game, MacSwain might win enough to teach the other a sound lesson, though never send the victim away from the table penniless. And in a case when a desperate man's need was apparent and without doubt, MacSwain had many times deliberately lost, doing it so cleverly the fact was never apparent to anyone but himself.

Quick in his judgment, he could know swift liking for another man on first meeting, as had been the case with Chris Waddell, or to know equally swift dislike, even hatred, his plesent feeling toward Price Ringgold.

Like most of his kind he was superstitious, and where his instincts were concerned, trusted them fully. And with Price Ringgold, these instincts slugged him solidly. He despised the pale eyed, tawny Ringgold, who showed so little and hid so much behind that secretive half-smile which could so swiftly become a set snarl when its owner was defied or his arrogance tossed back in his face.

Toward Byron A. Garrison and Lamar Hume, MacSwain's feeling was completely neutral. He knew no qualms at taking their money, for they were mature men who enjoyed the game. And if, too often, they tried to substitute the weight of a bet for a proper judgment of the percentages of chance, they could afford to pay for the mistake.

He had finished his brandy and was lighting another cigar when Scotty Deale faced him across the bar and jerked an indicating nod.

'They're waitin' for you.'

132

MacSwain showed his brief smile. 'So I notice. But after last night and being new in this camp, I'm wondering about your feelings toward me and my trade?'

Scotty Deale shrugged. 'Suits me so long as you deal 'em halfway fair. Fact is, I been thinkin' of bringing in a house man. Later on, maybe, we might get together.'

'Perhaps,' MacSwain murmured.

He sauntered over to the poker table where Byron A. Garrison and Lamar Hume were seated, Garrison waiting stolidly, Lamar Hume restlessly laying out dummy hands. Price Ringgold held a place toward the far end of the bar, but as soon as MacSwain approached the poker table moved up to it himself.

MacSwain did not miss the quickness of this move, nor did he miss the hungry glint in those pale eyes, facts which he checked away in the back of his mind for future use. Ringgold was definitely one of the greedy ones, whose avidity could lead to reckless plunging. To Hume and Garrison the gambler's nod was affable.

'Gentlemen! You are looking for revenge?'

'Not the right word,' said Garrison with some pompousness. 'Rather, a chance to get even.'

Lamar Hume showed a short, quick laugh. 'With me it's that I just plain hate like hell to lose. At poker, or anything else.'

He was a taut man, full of a driving

restlessness that made him appear nervous and edgy. But his glance was level and steady, and, as man to man, MacSwain's judgment rated him above Garrison.

'Show me one who says he likes to lose and I'll show you one who is either a fool or a liar,' the gambler observed. He turned and laid a cool glance on Price Ringgold. 'And you?'

Ringgold's reply was curt, told nothing. 'Let's get started.'

'Let's!' agreed MacSwain, equally curt.

Over on Ute Street, Chris Waddell paced out the deepening night hours on solitary patrol. The distant gunshot which be investigated, came to nothing. Probably, he decided, some cowhand from the hill range round about, letting off steam by throwing a shot at the stars.

Despite the threat of the night, Waddell moved along Ute Street with growing confidence, as alert observation made for increasing familiarity with the physical makeup of the Gulch, which in turn enabled him to watch all angles with greater certainty.

There was the usual crop of drunks and near drunks to cajole and steer back toward their sleeping quarters on wavering uncertain steps. He broke up two more fights that were getting out of hand and headed off several arguments that showed signs of turning into something much worse.

He stopped in at the Staghorn, where he

met and held Breed Garvey's wicked glare until the dive owner's glance wavered and he turned back to his bar chores, the marks of the gun-whipping he'd taken last night still livid across his face.

Further survey of the deadfall showed a poker game going on in a far corner. One of the players was Jack Millerson's clerk, Spence Munger, who was so intent on the cards he was unaware of Waddell's presence. Standing behind Munger's chair, watching the play, was the same rusty haired rider who carried one arm in a sling and had been in the place last night to growl his protest when Waddell laid his gun barrel across Breed Garvey's face. Neither of them noticed Waddell as he studied them for a musing moment or two before returning to the street.

The first time he came even with Hogan Geer's Belle Union deadfall, Waddell did not pause. Here was the headquarters of the thing he was combating, the thing that could destroy him. And there were those, it seemed, who were willing to wager that it would. It was aglow with light and full of the rumble of men's voices. As Waddell went by, every faculty in him was bright and singing with a taut alertness.

Fifty yards along he stopped and looked back. No one was following him, and so far as he could see there were no skulkers about. He shook his head impatiently, almost angrily.

135

This wouldn't do—wouldn't do at all. Not to figuratively hold his breath and walk on tiptoe every time he passed the damn place. The pressure should never be on him, but on the other side. On Geer and his bully boys.

A short byway, more alley than street, broke off Ute toward the east hill flank of the Gulch. It was a narrow, furtive place, full of uneasy half-gloom. When even with it, Waddell heard a man and woman arguing heatedly. Sounded a curse, a slapping blow and a muffled cry of pain, followed by the scurry of movement as the woman ran into view, holding a hand to her face. She dodged past Waddell and stopped in the beam of light from a window, where she stood looking back into the shadows.

Out of these a man charged, still cursing. With the hooking sweep of a foot, Waddell cut the legs from under the fellow, dropping him with a crash, where he lay, knocked breathless.

'Stay there!' Waddell ordered harshly. He turned to the woman. 'What's all the trouble?'

She had taken her hand from her face and in the frugal light glow he saw a minor stain of blood, seeping from one corner of her mouth. She stared at him, sullen and hard as nails. Without answering, she marched back into the shadows.

Waddell dug a boot toe into the man. 'Get up and get out!'

The fellow scrambled to his feet, showed a

surly snarl and slunk away.

Ute Street!

It was nearing midnight when Chris Waddell's next patrol found him in front of the Belle Union again. He paused, staring at the door. Sooner or later, Waddell, he told himself, you got to go through that door—alone! You'll never be boss of this damn street until you do. And so long as you must—well—!

Decision formed abruptly. He shouldered open the door and went in.

At one end of the bar was a railed off enclosure, just large enough to hold a poker table and a couple of chairs. Directly above hung one of the several lamps of the big bar and gambling room. Its cone of yellow light glinted on the bald, bony skull of Hogan Geer as he sat in one of the chairs, a drink on the table at his elbow, a half burned cigar in his small, tight mouth.

His black, cold eyes constantly roved the room. Nor did his restless glance miss any flicker of the swinging door when someone entered or left the place. So it was that the moment Chris Waddell appeared, Geer saw him.

Once through the door, Waddell paused to make his survey of the place. It came presently to Hogan Geer and settled there. He moved up, swung open the small wicket of the railed enclosure and stepped through. Geer's cold, toneless drone bit at him.

'Nobody comes through that wicket unless I ask them too. I didn't ask you.'

'No,' agreed Waddell curtly, 'you didn't. Yet I'm here, with something to say to you.'

'Maybe I don't want to listen.'

'Maybe you better. It concerns your hide. Whether you want to keep it whole.'

Hogan Geer whipped forward in his chair.

'Why damn you! You'd threaten me in my own place?'

'I might,' Waddell told him stonily, 'even twist your neck. Better hold still, Geer.'

The dive owner stared up at him. 'You got something to say, let's have it!'

'It's this,' Waddell told him. 'The Spooner brothers are your dogs. Maybe you got others who are the same; I don't know about that. What I do know is this. The Spooners threw some talk my way today, rough talk. Now somebody has circulated the word that I won't last the night. So far I've been doing pretty good. If you got the Spooners laying for me somewhere, better call them off, Geer. Because I don't kill easy and I fight for keeps. And I'll hold you responsible. Am I understood?'

Geer did not answer, just seemed to crouch a little lower in his chair, small and venomous.

Waddell waited through a long half minute for any reply from Hogan Geer, but when none came, turned away and made a complete

138

steady circuit of the crowded room before stepping once more into the outer night.

Occupying a place of honor in the very center of the bottle shelf behind the Palace Bar, was a wide-faced Sessions clock. Its case was of dark walnut which time and use had coated an almost black patina and its brass trim and bindings were tarnished. But its works were still sound and it struck off every hour and half hour of the day and night in deep, mellow tones.

It tolled out the hour now, in twelve measured notes. Midnight. On the final stroke, Price Ringgold, pale eyes glittering with banked anger and frustration, shoved his chair violently back from the poker table, surged to his feet and stood glaring across at Ace MacSwain. There were no chips in front of Ringgold. There were a lot of them in front of MacSwain.

'No man,' Ringgold burst out, 'can have that kind of luck legitimately. MacSwain, you're just another damn tinhorn!'

Ace MacSwain's face turned smooth and bland and expressionless. He too pushed back his chair and got to his feet.

'Not luck,' he said, quietly even. 'Just know-how. Legitimate know-how. When you infer more than that, Ringgold—you lie!'

Scotty Deale, watching and listening, came around the end of the bar swiftly.

'Easy does it, gents! I want no trouble in

here.'

Lamar Hume looked at Ringgold with angry disgust.

'If you can't play without losing like a gentlemen, Ringgold, don't play at all! And I'd remind you that I dealt that last hand. You owe MacSwain an apology. I want to hear it. If I don't, you'll never sit into another poker game with me!'

Byron A. Garrison shifted uncomfortably in his chair. He also had lost considerably and didn't particularly like it. But in support of his somewhat pompous dignity, he echoed Hume's words.

'There was no basis for your charge, Price. I would hear you admit it.'

'Yes,' murmured Ace MacSwain. 'And now!'

None of them heard Chris Waddell enter, who got the picture at a glance.

'Would there be a disagreement?'

They came around to face him. Ace MacSwain answered.

'Ringgold would excuse his own poor playing by charging that I manipulated the cards. I'm waiting for him to retract.'

'So am I!' snapped Lamar Hume.

Although Ace MacSwain was an acquaintance of but a few short days, Chris Waddell felt he had come to know the man rather well. He could see that the gambler's sense of personal honor was outraged, and that behind his bland, almost too quiet

140

attitude, a deep anger was simmering.

Waddell looked at Byron A. Garrison. 'What is your feeling?'

Garrison cleared his throat bruskly. 'I saw nothing out of order.'

Waddell put his glance on Price Ringgold.

'There you have it. You seem to be out-voted, three to one. And when you accuse a man of cheating at cards you be damn sure of your ground, for that kind of talk can lead to gunplay. I suggest you apologize!'

'No!' Ringgold blurted. 'I—!'

'Yes!' cut in Waddell harshly.

Ringgold flared furiously. 'Keep out of this! It's none of your affair. I know what I'm do—.'

'I'm making it my affair,' Waddell cut in again. 'It's my business to head off trouble. You're wrong, Ringgold—and you know it. Be man enough to admit it.'

'I admit nothing, I retract nothing,' Ringgold stormed. 'To me a tinhorn is a tinhorn and never anything better. As for you—!'

'Yes?' cut in Waddell a third time. 'What about me?'

He moved ahead a little as he spoke, the challenge unmistakable. Startled, Ringgold backed away, went quickly quiet. After which he stepped past Waddell, heading for the door and through it.

Silence held for a time. Then Byron A. Garrison spoke, somewhat stiffly.

141

'Ringgold is my man, and in the main a valuable one. Tonight he was wrong. I apologize for him.'

'Generous of you,' acknowledged Ace MacSwain. 'I am sorry the evening had to end this way.'

As on the previous night, Waddell and Ace MacSwain left the Palace together. On the street they paused, side by side, still for a little time. Then MacSwain spoke quietly.

'That fellow Ringgold lied, of course.'

'I'm sure of it,' Waddell agreed.

'You shut him up, quick.'

'Aimed to and was glad of the chance. I don't like his kind, not at all. They're basically pirates, buccaneers. They understand only one language.'

'That would be a toughness greater than their own?' MacSwain suggested.

'Yes. You put the pressure on them and you keep it there.'

'And wait for the shot from the dark?'

Waddell shrugged. 'I know of a fellow breaking his neck by falling out of a buckboard. Nobody pushed him, either.'

MacSwain laughed softly. 'The perfect philosophy. You're through for the night?'

'I figured on one more look at Ute.'

'Mind if I go along? I need the walk and the air.'

'You'll gain no friends, being seen with me,' Waddell warned.

142

'I'll be walking with one. To hell with the rest.'

The edge was off the night's activity. The growl of Ute Street had dwindled to a murmur, its lights dimming and going out. A few late loiterers were in evidence, but after its earlier turbulence the street seemed empty. Midnight, apparently, along Ute, was the hour of change.

In the past Chris Waddell had known other wild streets like this one, but they had all been in cattle towns where, at midnight, the hour was still considered comparatively early. But Midas Hill was a mining camp, and most of those who sought the pleasures of Ute Street were due on shift at the mines in the morning.

Back on Summit Street again, Ace MacSwain sighed his relief.

'There's a streak of steel in you, my friend. I couldn't stand the threat of that street, myself. It's there, all around you, like a feral odor.'

Waddell smiled thinly. 'Suppose we say it's no place for too-active imagination.'

'Don't you feel it—the threat?'

'Of course. But it's part of the job. You take on a job, then you take all it offers, the good and the bad.'

'That,' acknowledged MacSwain, 'is so. Well, it seems you've confounded the smart ones who were willing to wager against your chances. May they continue to lose!'

CHAPTER NINE

Doctor Jethro Stone had an office three doors along from the Hill House Hotel. He was stout and broad and square of face, brusk and direct in manner and speech; a man long practiced in his profession in a frontier world where physical hazard was a daily risk and violence more than casually present. So it was that most of the cases he was called on to attend were emergencies of some sort. He had sharp blue eyes which regarded Chris Waddell steadily from under frowning, bushy brows.

'Yes,' he growled, 'I recall such a man as you describe. He had a surface wound high on the left arm. Claimed he'd run into a snag in the timber. I had neither time nor inclination to argue the point with him. But I've seen snag wounds before; also those caused by a bullet. There's a difference. And this fellow had been shot. He had all the ear-marks of a rascal. Was he one?'

'I'm pretty sure he got the wound while attempting a hold-up,' Waddell said.

'Then,' rumbled Doctor Jethro Stone bluntly, 'it's too bad somebody didn't make a better job of it. My sympathies reach only to the decent and law-abiding. I've none to waste on the other sort.'

'My feelings, Doctor,' Waddell nodded,

moving to the door. 'I'm obliged to you.'

'Any time,' was the gruff reply. 'You're new in this camp and I understand you're both forceful and reckless. Don't be too much of the last, for we need your kind around.'

'You can't be much of the one without being some of the other, Doctor. Where did you hear such things of me?' Doctor Stone smiled grimly. 'I had supper last night with my good friends, Mike and Norma Vespasian. Among other things, you were an item of conversation.'

Dry humor touched Waddell's lips. 'So long as it is the good people who rake me over the coals, I don't mind. Again, thanks!'

Outside the doctor's office, mid-morning sun greeted him. He strode through it, crossing Summit Street at a long angle to Jack Millerson's store and trading post. In here his first swift glance searched for Norma Vespasian, but she was nowhere present. In a far corner young Spence Munger and Millerson's older clerk, Dad Weyl, were checking some shelf supplies, while Millerson himself was waiting on a town housewife who presently left with a basket of groceries over her arm. Millerson turned to Waddell, his manner somewhat more cordial than previously.

'Just a couple of questions,' Waddell explained briefly. 'That young fellow yonder—how long has he worked for you?'

'You mean Spence Munger? Maybe six or eight months. Why?' Millerson frowned his puzzlement.

'Wondering. The sack of specie Miss Vespasian brought in for you—who besides you and her knew she was bringing it?'

Millerson looked startled. 'Why—nobody outside of this store.'

'Did Munger know about it?'

'Yes. Any reason why he shouldn't have?'

'I'll let you be the judge of that,' Waddell said. 'I don't know a damn thing except what I see, understand. But I did see Munger playing poker in Breed Garvey's deadfall last night, and standing alongside his chair was a certain shifty cowhand with one arm in a sling. First time I patrolled Ute Street—when I argued with Garvey, this same cowhand was there. I had cause to ask him what was wrong with his arm. He claimed his bronc threw him and broke it. Well, I just came from Doc Stone's office. It was Doc who fixed that fellow up. Doc said he'd been shot, though with Doc he claimed he'd run into a snag in heavy timber. Do you begin to get a picture?'

'I do if I accept your insinuation concerning Spence Munger. Which I don't!' Millerson's tone ran sharp. 'I can trust Spence. He's a good boy,'

'Now I hope so,' Waddell drawled. 'But such things can be a matter of opinion. Millerson, there had to be some way for word of that

146

specie to get out, because the hold up hombre was set and certain of it. I've given you an angle to think on. If you come up with anything better, let me know.'

He would have turned away, but Millerson stopped him with an outstretched hand.

'Wait a minute! What you're trying to say is that this stray cowhand with an arm in a sling is the fellow who tried to make that holdup at Grizzly Spring. And because he and Spence Munger were in Garvey's deadfall together, it was Spence who tipped him off about the specie. Is that it?'

'I'm not saying anything for positive,' Waddell retorted. 'I'm just reading sign as I run, and suggesting where it seems to lead. So that you can be forewarned in the future.'

Millerson laid a long, speculative glance on Spence Munger and Dad Weyl. He shook his head as though in violent denial of something.

'Dad Weyl has been with me for years. I'd trust him with my last dollar—and my life. I mean that.'

'We weren't talking about the old chap,' reminded Waddell. 'I know how you feel, Millerson. You just hate to believe someone you've trusted isn't worthy of it. I could be wrong, understand—way wrong. I hope I am. But—human nature being what it is—and a lot of it isn't exactly pretty, well, a man would be foolish not to be practical.'

'Yes,' agreed Millerson reluctantly. 'That is

so. I'll keep a more alert eye on things. And I appreciate your bother and concern.'

Waddell waved a casual hand. 'Part of the job. Something else that isn't any of my business, maybe—but what kind of a salary do you pay Munger?'

'A fair one. Certainly enough to live on comfortably.'

'And to gamble on?'

Millerson's glance narrowed. 'Why?'

'The game Munger was sitting in on last night wasn't for nickels.'

Millerson considered this for a moment, then swore softly.

'Damn you, Waddell—damn you!' But, when Waddell turned toward the door, Millerson slapped him on the shoulder as he passed.

From Millerson's, Chris Waddell went along Summit Street with quick, vigorous strides, an eagerness stirring in him. The two items of concern he'd decided upon last evening had been taken care of. There were no further responsibilities ahead of him until nightfall; the balance of the daylight hours were his to do with as he pleased, and he knew exactly what he wanted those hours to hold.

At the corrals he looked up Tim Roach, a leathery, taciturn Irishman and within another fifteen minutes was sitting in a rented saddle astride a rented horse and climbing out of the Midas Hill basin to the north. Within a mile it was as though Midas Hill had never been. Here was timber on every hand, fir and pine and tamarack, with aspen showing every now and then.

Here also, but for the ruffle of jogging hoofs, the somewhat raucous, yet not unpleasant melody of a stellar jay, and the more distant chatter of a pair of pine squirrels, was a silence and a solitude that he savored hungrily. Here was something he needed, a refuge from Ute Street and all that it held.

It was the first time he had been in a saddle since the days of Mesa Bluffs. The mount under him was a good one, strong and easy-gaited. Going nowhere in particular and with plenty of time for the going, he let the horse have its own will and way and so fell presently into a trail leading off to the north, skirting timbered points and slopes, topping low ridges and crossing little flats and meadows which broke through now and then.

The trail held hoof sign to show that others had been over it recently, and Waddell pondered this fact idly before putting it aside and giving himself over completely to the pleasure of traveling through this country without care or effort. Somewhat later and several miles along he moved into a meadow and there faced another rider. Waddell reined in and touched his hat.

'Miss Vespesian!'

Norma Vespasian's glance held his levelly.

149

'This,' she said, 'is a surprise. I had not expected to meet a man like you outside the limits of Midas Hill.'

Chris Waddell had been half smiling, almost boyishly eager. Now came a quick withdrawing, a sobering which hardened him and made him remote.

'A man like me, eh?' he murmured, his tone dryly curt. 'You see me as something strange, something apart from the rest of the human race?'

She flushed slightly. 'I spoke poorly. I did not mean it so. But that badge you carry—its responsibilities—?'

'Have claim on me only at night,' Waddell said. 'The day belongs to someone else.'

'To Frank Scorbie? Where it means nothing?'

'That may be,' Waddell admitted. 'Yet—still his day. Me, I'm here to get away from Ute Street for a little time.'

He broke out his smoking and she watched him fashion a cigarette.

'You realize, of course, that you've become a person of considerable note in Midas Hill?'

He slanted a quick glance at her, wondering at the remark. She was dressed in a divided skirt and a man's wool shirt, with silk scarf about her throat to add a bit of color. She wore her clothes well and she sat easy and straight in her saddle. Under the steadiness of his regard color again touched her cheeks.

'You must be mistaken,' he drawled. 'I'm really a very ordinary fellow.'

'Not from all I hear. It has taken you only a couple of days to build a reputation for making the law mean what it says. I'm wondering if the reputation will last.' There was challenge in the words.

Waddell touched a match to his cigarette and inhaled deeply.

'Such as it is, it will last,' he said briefly. 'I accepted a month's pay, so a month I serve. After that I don't know. It could depend on what develops. As it stands, the man who hired me, Frank Scorbie, would now like to fire me. I won't let him. So you see me as a sort of renegade, with few friends in Midas Hill and little chance of making more.'

'Is it just the month's pay that keeps you here? There are no other reasons?'

He mused over that, his eyes narrowed, his lips set in a slight pull of cynical pondering. Presently he nodded.

'Yes, there are other reasons. You might say the element of pride enters. Also, a man in my trade can't afford to let himself be pushed around, or let a street like Ute whip him. He can't afford to run away. Once he starts, he's through. It makes no difference how far he runs, or where. Once he does he can never live it down. Particularly with himself. Which is bound to leave him a lot less man than he was.'

'Like Frank Scorbie?'

151

'Like Frank Scorbie,' Waddell agreed slowly. 'Frank started to run, and now he can't stop. It's too bad. Once he was a good man—a mighty good man. One of the best.'

In his words there was a note of real regret, which brought a swift warming into Norma Vespasian's glance.

'I think,' she said steadily, 'I'm beginning to understand you just a little, Chris Waddell.'

'Why then,' he said swiftly, 'I'm glad we both happened to be on the same trail this morning. Now, if you don't mind, it's my turn to wonder. Over what brings you out here?'

She explained simply. 'My father went back to his cattle camp at Alpine Meadows early this morning. I rode with him as far as the Heron Creek glades. You see, I too like to get away from Midas Hill whenever I can.'

'That could be my good luck. Is there any reason why we can't ride back together?'

Again she measured him with that clear, candid glance, and the glimmerings of a faint, sweet smile pulled at her lips.

'I can't think of any good one.'

'Fine!' enthused Waddell, swinging his horse around. 'This makes it a really great day.'

They jogged along side by side and it was Norma Vespasian who first broke the silence.

'Mr. Waddell, is there any reason why Spence Munger should dislike you?'

Waddell looked at her. 'Make that Chris, and I'll answer you.'

Color once more touched her cheek, but she did not hedge,

'Very well—Chris.'

'Munger,' said Waddell, 'he's Millerson's clerk. I've spoken to him just once, which was yesterday when I was in the store to buy a coat. He waited on me. Right now I can't think of anything I said or did to make him dislike me. Unless he just doesn't like the cut of my jib. That can happen, you know. You meet somebody. Something about them goes against the grain. So—,' shrugging, 'you just don't like them.' He considered a moment, then added, 'Why are you concerned? Or isn't it any of my business?'

'I'm not too sure it's really any of my business,' came the somewhat reluctant answer. 'It's about what happened at Grizzly Spring. I've wondered ever since how any holdup could have learned that I'd be bringing in specie and that I'd be riding with Barney Guilfoyle instead of on a stage. Definite word had to get out. But how? Only we who work in the store knew about it.'

'Ah!' exclaimed Waddell to the world at large. 'The lady now proves that she is not only exceedingly good to look at, but also exceedingly smart. Go on, Miss Vespasian— say more. You interest me very much.'

'*Miss* Vespasian?' She cocked a brow.

Waddell grinned. 'Sorry. I was afraid to before. Go on, Norma. Because I am interested—very!'

'All right. Now I know I told no one. I'm sure Mr. Millerson didn't, and I know Dad Weyl wouldn't.'

'Which leaves Spence Munger,' Waddell murmured. 'That's it, isn't it?'

Norma sighed. 'I'm afraid so. And I don't know why I should think it.'

Waddell took a final deep drag on his cigarette, crushed the butt to dust on his saddle horn.

'You think it,' he declared, 'because it is the one angle that makes the most sense. Maybe I can help you out. Did you know that Spence Munger bucked the tiger?'

'I've suspected that he did. But then, most men gamble to some extent.'

'True. But it all depends. Now last night I saw Munger in a game in Breed Garvey's dive. And like I told Jack Millerson, you don't play for fun in a place like that.'

Startled, she twisted in her saddle to half face Waddell. 'You've spoken to Mr. Millerson—about Spence?'

'Yes. Before I left town this morning.'

'Why did you?'

'It's like this. I've done my share of wondering about that holdup attempt, too. Along the lines you mention. This we know. Somebody must have talked. Why? The oldest reason in the world for a thing of that sort is the hope of easy money—or some quick need

154

for it. Bucking the tiger has put many a man in that shape.

'Now it happens that a certain tough, surly saddle-hand hangs out in Breed Garvey's deadfall. Right now he has one arm in a sling. Doc Stone tells me he fixed up a bullet wound in that arm. And last night the owner of that arm was right at Spence Munger's elbow, watching the poker game.'

'You're saying that proves something?'

'Not saying it does, but suggesting that it might,' Waddell corrected. 'Suggesting that Munger and the saddle-hand could be more than complete strangers. When you've been adding up this, and wondering about that, you learn to take note of such angles and consider their possibilities. And now there's more. You suggest that Spence Munger appears to dislike me. Again—why? For lack of a better reason, could it be because he lost out in a holdup payoff that didn't pan out as planned? And because I happened to be the one who busted up the holdup attempt by being present and throwing a bullet that chewed a hole in a certain individual's arm? There, Norma Vespasian, are some questions worth thinking on!'

She stared at him, wide-eyed and distressed.

'You really think that is the way and why of it?'

He tipped a shrugging shoulder. 'Call it a theory. But men have been hung on less.'

She looked away, biting her lip. 'Poor Spence!' she murmured. Then she turned back on Waddell a trifle fiercely. 'I'm not sure I like you, Chris Waddell. You have a suspicious mind.'

He chuckled. 'Whereby the lady proves herself the eternally feminine. When the wisdom of the mind meets up with emotion of the heart, wisdom suffers.'

She tossed her head. 'I did not know you were a philosopher.'

Waddell chuckled again. 'In my trade a man has to have some touch of the philosopher in his makeup. Otherwise he never would come up with any answers.'

Once more they rode in silence. Then Norma Vespasian again murmured: 'Poor Spence!'

Waddell looked at her. 'Don't waste your sympathies. Oh, I know how you feel. You work in the same store as he does, you've probably considered him as a friend. Yet there's only one way to look at it. If Munger is entirely innocent, there's no point in feeling sorry for him. On the other hand, if he has tried to sell out Jack Millerson, the man paying his wages, then he isn't worth a single regret. Also—,' here Waddell's tone harshened, 'if he had anything to do with that holdup attempt, then he certainly wasn't concerned over your welfare!'

She considered for a moment. 'Perhaps not,'

she admitted gravely. 'All you say is true enough. Still, there are those in the world who are somehow so forlorn. Their appearance thwarts them, ability, or rather the lack of it, thwarts them, and so, perhaps in time sheer frustration turns them desperate and they do things without thinking of the consequences . . .'

'That could be,' Waddell acknowledged. 'Certainly there are plenty of causes for tears in the world. Yet, if man is to live together under conditions reasonably better than a jungle, then laws must be observed and respected and rights protected. Such things are basic. And the Spence Mungers of the world must live up to the rules the same as the rest.'

Again she twisted in her saddle to study him. 'Did I say philosopher? You really hate those outside the law, don't you?'

'They are the enemy!' Waddell declared flatly. 'And a crook is a crook because he likes the idea. In which case, when he meets up with the penalty, he's got nobody to blame but himself. And I never saw one of the breed yet who objected to the idea of a law man being put out of the way. Maybe the feeling is hate. I know it was how old Dan Wheelock, the sheriff who first pinned a deputy's badge on me, taught me to feel. And Dan Wheelock was just about the best, and most widely respected law officer I ever knew.'

'You are,' she said, 'disturbingly convincing. And, I'm afraid, convincingly right.'

'Fair enough,' he smiled. 'With that settled, what say we make the most of pleasant time and pleasant company and forget Spence Munger for a while?'

*   *   *

In Hogan Geer's Belle Union deadfall it was the dead hour of the day, the opening hour. The barroom was empty except for a swamper pushing a broom across a floor littered with the inevitable refuse. Mine sump mud, and dust and dirt from hillside and street, scuffed from the careless boots of men. Soggy half-chewed cigar butts, cold and stagnant and trampled. Shards of several shattered whiskey glasses; remnants of a Paddy's blackened clay pipe. A filthy, tattered bandana handkerchief and a sweat and dirt crusted hat which some drunk had lost, these also trampled and ground down into the rest of the refuse.

Doors were propped wide to let out the stale and rancid odors of the night before. Bitter ghosts of a hundred dead cigars and pipes. The sweet-sour breath of spilled whiskey, and back of it all the strange, heavy, animal-den jungle reek of crowded and unwashed humans.

A lone barkeep moved up and down, dull and lethargic, his mind cluttered and smothered by lack of sleep and good air. With half-hearted, mechanical effort he wiped down

158

the bar, washed and stacked glasses. He came upon a near empty whiskey bottle, eyed it, lifted it and drained it. He shuddered, stretched and tightened his lips against the bite of the liquor, blinked his blood-shot eyes. He tossed the empty bottle into a box under the bar, where it made a small, breaking crash.

Price Ringgold came in from the street. The suggestion of felineness in this man, occasioned by his pale, hard-staring eyes, his tawniness of coloring, was heightened by a certain fastidiousness in manner and dress. Even his soft, prowling step held something cat-like.

He went quickly along the length of the room, ignoring both swamper and bartender. He did not knock at the rear door, just opened it and stepped through. Five men were in the back room ahead of him. Hogan Geer, Breed Garvey and the three Spooner brothers. Garvey gave out with a surly growl.

'You're late. We been waitin' near an hour. I could have used that extra sleep.'

Garvey's face was still grotesque from the effects of the pistol whipping administered by Chris Waddell, and past the swelling and discoloring bruises his eyes were small, hot, pit-bottom fires.

An answering heat showed briefly in Ringgold's stare. Then he tipped a dismissing shoulder. 'There were mining affairs to take care of. Also, Garrison had me by the ear and

159

wouldn't let go.'

'Well, we're all here now,' Hogan Geer said. 'So let's get about settling several things. First, this Chris Waddell. Seems Scorbie can't handle him, so we'll have to.'

'Scorbie!' Ringgold spat the name like he might a curse. 'That useless sot!'

'Just so,' nodded Geer in his cold, humorless way. 'But useful to us because he is useless. He's a front, and don't count beyond that. Which is all we want of the marshal's office. Sure, he made a mistake in bringing in Waddell. He guessed wrong, there. But so did the rest of us. Now it's up to us to do something about it. You got any ideas?'

Ringgold indicated the Spooners. 'There's your chore boys. Have they taken on religion?'

'Hardly,' Geer retorted drily. 'And available if necessary.'

'Well, then?'

Geer shook his naked head. 'It's not quite that simple. Even though Waddell has only been here a few days he's got the whole damn camp talking about him. He's a tough proposition, that fellow—as tough as they come.'

'He's mortal,' Ringgold said shortly. 'And a shot from the dark—!' He shrugged.

'Again, not that simple,' Geer said. 'A shot, yes—but not from the dark. Anything like that would point straight at the Gulch. Which we can't afford.'

160

Ringgold's pale stare sharpened. 'What are you talking about, Geer? What can't the Gulch afford? You turning soft, or something?'

'No. Just smart.' Geer leaned back in his chair, gnawed the tip from a cheroot and lit it. Past the first mouthful of smoke he resumed. 'Here's a picture. Try and get it. In my time I've seen a dozen camps like this one start up, grow, live, and in many cases, die. In all of them, when the first big rush and fever went on, then nobody gave much of a damn about anything. And men like you and me and Breed here, cashed in big! But the human animal is a peculiar brute. Basically he has an instinct for law and order, and sooner or later that instinct begins to show. This is a pretty rough camp. But there's been a hundred rougher ones in the past, and in everyone of them there came a time when fellows like you and me and Breed here moved on. That is, they did if they were smart.'

'Or scared?' jeered Ringgold.

Geer straightened and his words fell thin and edged.

'That's poor talk, Ringgold—not smart, not smart at all! Me, sure I'm scared any time it's intelligent to be scared. Only a damn fool wouldn't be. You? Any marks of your teeth in Waddell's hide? I understand you had your chance to put some there. Like in the Palace, last night. Well?'

Ringgold flushed. 'All right. You're not

161

scared. You're just being smart. This law and order talk—there's something behind it. Let's have it.'

Mollified, Hogan Geer settled back in his chair again.

'Like I said, it takes time for any camp to find itself. But one day—some certain man comes along to bring that instinct for law and order into focus, and to provide a rallying point. This fellow Waddell could be just such a man.'

'All the more reason to get rid of him then,' said Ringgold.

'I go along with you there,' Geer agreed. 'But not on Ute Street. It mustn't happen on Ute Street. If possible, not even near Ute Street.'

'Why not on Ute?'

Hogan Geer made a gesture of impatience.

'I just told you. The law and order instinct. It's beginning to rumble in this camp. Not loud as yet, but if you listen real careful you can hear it. It's like a charge of dynamite, harmless until something comes along to set it off. Maybe it never does explode, but it's smart to remember that the ingredients are always there.'

He took a deep drag at his cheroot, then took it from his lips and waved it up and down to emphasize his next remark.

'I figure this camp has about another year, maybe even eighteen months to really boom.

And I want to ride that boom to the finish because there's lots of good money to be made. But let's be frank about some facts. Nobody likes our methods but us. The fools sweat for their money the hard way. We take it away from them in a lot of, for us, easy ways. They know that we do it, but they keep coming back because they got no other place to go, not because they like us. And that mass dislike is the charge of dynamite we got to consider all the time, and plan according. Which is why, while we got to get rid of Waddell, it has to be done in a way that won't point the finger at Ute Street.'

Price Ringgold turned thoughtful. He nodded slowly.

'You make sense,' he acknowledged. 'You also make the chore of getting rid of Waddell no easier. Unless you've figured something out?'

Hogan Geer tipped his head toward Breed Garvey. 'Me and Breed, we have.'

'Good enough. But before you tell me about it, here's something I want done.'

'What is it?'

'Not what—who,' Ringgold said. 'That tinhorn MacSwain, who hit town a couple of days ago and is playing in the Palace.'

'So-o! What's he done to you?'

Ringgold flared. 'Does it matter?'

'Not particularly. Though a man does wonder.' For the first time, Hogan Geer's cold,

163

expressionless manner broke enough to let through the faint shadow of a smile. 'How much did he win from you, Price?'

'Too damn much!' Ringgold rapped hotly.

'While also cutting in on your own private sucker preserve, Mister Hume and Mister Garrison?'

'So long as you ask—yes! Anything else?'

Hogan Geer's tight lips twitched again. 'No. What do you want done with MacSwain?'

'I want him out of this camp. I don't care how it's done, just so it's done right and for good. Or will that turn loose this law and order business you're afraid of?'

Hogan Geer shook his head. 'I don't think so. Nobody gives much of a damn about just another tinhorn.' He turned to Elvie Spooner. 'You heard what Price wants done. Take care of it.'

'For your trouble,' put in Ringgold, 'his pockets should be lined. In two nights of play he's taken five hundred from me. I know he's into Garrison for at least that much or more. And he's nicked Hume pretty heavy, too. All you find on him is yours if you do a real job.'

Raw avarice glittered in the eyes of Elvie Spooner.

'Me and Lee and Buff—we'll do a job!' he promised.

Price Ringgold put his glance on Hogan Geer again. 'Now,' he demanded, 'what's this you and Garvey got figured for Waddell?'

CHAPTER TEN

It had been another tough night for Frank Scorbie, and with nothing left but the cold dregs of the whiskey he had taken on, even a new day's bright morning sunlight flooding through the window above his bunk failed to dispel the gray curse of his thoughts. His mouth was foul, his face bloated and scummed with beard stubble.

He cleaned up after a fashion, shaving with cold water, and what with the general all-over shakiness of his condition, succeeded in nicking himself several times. His queasy stomach needed settling, but the whiskey bottle lying on the floor by the bunk was empty, so his thoughts turned to the hot coffee in Frenchy's hashhouse across the street.

He stepped out into the morning somewhat furtively, a man filled with a sodden shame which made him reluctant to face either the world or the people in it. Mild activity stirred along Summit Street and this Scorbie surveyed with blurred and bloodshot eyes. When his glance swung toward the lower end he saw the spare, tall figure of Chris Waddell emerge from Millerson's store and stride vigorously off to Tim Roach's livery and freight corrals. Continuing to watch he presently saw Waddell ride out of town astride a solid looking grullo mount.

For a moment it struck him that Waddell might be leaving Midas Hill for good. Second thought, however, denied this. A man needed considerable money to buy a horse like that, and Waddell did not have that kind of money in his pocket.

Three big mugs of Frenchy's black coffee helped so much, Scorbie added a fairly substantial breakfast to them and as a consequence returned to the street feeling considerably better. Except for the memory of the poorly concealed contempt which showed in Frenchy's eyes when he set out the coffee and the food.

Damn them, Scorbie thought, weakly savage. Damn them all! They want the town left wide open for the sake of business, then sneer at me because I run it that way . . .

He felt his pockets for a cigar, found none, so crossed to the office in the hope of locating one there. Buff Spooner sat behind the desk, leaning far back in a chair, his feet cocked up.

'Pretty soft!' he jeered. 'Nothing to do but lay around, soak up whiskey and draw your pay. Yeah—pretty soft!'

'Don't need your opinion,' retorted Scorbie shortly. 'What the hell you hanging around here for?'

Buff Spooner lowered his boots to the floor and straightened up, his eyes pinched with a cruel scorn.

'Don't use that tone with me, Scorbie! A drunk like you, sportin' a fancy badge! I've a notion to take it away and make you eat it. And I'm here to tell you Geer wants to see you. Not tomorrow, either. Today—right away!'

Buff Spooner got to his feet, spat contemptuously on the floor and walked out.

Frank Scorbie leaned against the desk and something not far from a sobbing groan broke from his lips.

Where had his manhood gone? In which bottle had he finally drowned it? The fiftieth— the hundredth—? Why, there was a time when he'd have made such as Buff Spooner grovel in the dust like a whipped cur! Had it really been that way—once? Had he really been such a man? Or was it just a mocking phantasy . . . ?

Hogan Geer was alone in the back room of the Belle Union. He let Scorbie stand for a little time while studying him with a cold black glance. Finally he nodded toward a chair.

'You know where Gold Run is?'

'Heard of it,' Scorbie admitted. 'Somewhere south of here?'

'About ten or twelve miles. Was a placer rush there once. It didn't last. Now there's nothing left but a bar and trading post of sorts and a few cabins. Friend of mine, Charley Urbine, has the bar and store. You're heading down there for ten days or two weeks.'

Scorbie stared. 'Me—going to Gold Run?

167

What are you talking about? Why should I head for Gold Run to lay around for a couple of weeks?'

'Because I'm telling you to,' Geer said.

'But for what reason—?'

'I got reasons. Good ones. I've already sent word to Charley Urbine. He's expecting you. So—that is the way it will be.'

'If I just knew why—?'

'You don't need to know why. All you should be concerned about is that you've got a good thing here. Do as you're told and you'll still have it. Otherwise—!' Hogan Geer let the threat hang.

Frank Scorbie swallowed thickly. 'If that's the way you want it, Hogan.'

'That's the way I want it. You can rent a horse from Tim Roach.'

Half an hour later, Frank Scorbie rode away from Midas Hill along a trail which led south through a broken country of wash and ravine and irregular rims. Past midday he came upon the meager weatherbeaten buildings of Gold Run clustered in a flat at the mouth of a wash that narrowly broke from the mountain face and let out some small creek waters. Crossing these, Scorbie's horse beat up a hollow echo on a log bridge, and the sound carried far enough to awaken signs of life among the buildings.

Two different men showed at the doors of cabins to have their quick look at Scorbie's

168

approach, then as quickly drift from sight. The largest building in the group, a cramped two-story affair with rough boarded walls and a roof of heavy, split stakes, was faced with a short run of rickety narrow porch. A lone chair graced this, holding a man who now got to his feet and turned from sight through the door beside him. Presently the door was filled by another man.

Filled literally. He who occupied it was enormously larded with fat. Fat which made misshapen, padded mounds of his shoulders, and his torso a gross, big-bellied mass. In a pear-shaped, heavily jowled face his eyes were small and slyly secretive. His lips were heavy, the lower one dropping. Coarse, sparse hair, pale as straw, stubbled his head.

Motionless he stood and motionless he watched as Scorbie hauled up and dismounted, stiff from unaccustomed miles in the saddle. Scorbie's glance roved for a moment before settling on the fat man.

'Where'll I find Urbine?'

'I'm Urbine.' The answer came in words that were moist and slow and breathy. 'You'll be Scorbie. Been expectin' you.' The fat man turned his bead slightly and lifted his thick voice. 'Spike!'

A man showed at the corner of the building.

'Take care of the horse,' Urbine ordered.

Spike led the animal away and Scorbie followed Urbine inside. The room was full of shadows. It held a short bar, a single poker table and some shelves piled with varied food supplies. At one end of the bar a narrow stairway led upwards. Urbine indicated this.

'First room at the top of the right should do you. A drink on the house?'

The words awakened an inner trembling eagerness in Frank Scorbie, but for some obscure reason beyond his own immediate fathoming, he shook his head.

'Not now.'

He climbed the stairs and turned out of a narrow hallway into the room at the right. The walls were bare and the floor was bare. The lone item of furniture was a bunk, roughly made up with worn, faded blankets. A single small window, long unwashed, let in light only thinly.

Scorbie sat on the bunk wearily. His shoulders drooped and he stared at the floor. Craving for whiskey made the saliva gather and flood his mouth, so that he swallowed convulsively. But in him was that strange and startling stubbornness which denied the liquor hunger, and presently, as this dulled and lessened, he stretched out on the bunk and went to sleep.

'You must have given Scorbie ideas. Only he'll be gone longer than you were.'

There was the touch of a faint but pungent sarcasm in the remark Tim Roach made as he took over the rein of the grullo bronc Chris

Waddell had been riding.

Chris Waddell stared. 'Given Scorbie ideas? He'll be gone longer than I was? I can't quite nail that down, friend. What do you mean?'

The corral owner shrugged. 'After you left this mornin', Scorbie hauled out, too.'

'Hauled out—for good?' demanded Waddell.

Tim Roach snorted. 'Not if he knows what's good for him. I only rented him that bronc, I didn't sell it to him. No, he said he'd be gone ten days or so.'

'Where to?'

'He didn't say. And not figgerin' it as any of my business, I didn't ask.' Roach gave Waddell a narrowed, slanting glance. 'Sort of leaves all the law up to you for a time, doesn't it?'

'Sort of!' closed out Waddell.

He went directly to the office. Wherever Frank Scorbie had gone, he'd done a fair job of mucking out the back room before he left. The bunk was made up and the floor swept after a fashion. Waddell went out front again and sat down at the desk and began going through it on the hope of finding some clue as to why and where.

He had no luck. The desk drawers were an untidy hodgepodge of this and that. A clutter of reward dodgers, most of them old, one or two fairly new. A saddle and boot catalogue. A broken spur and a loose handful of .45 Colt pistol cartridges. A partially emptied sack of

171

Durham tobacco, a thin book of brown wheat straw papers, and a crushed, dried out cigar. Some pencil stubs, a penholder without any point, and an ancient bottle of ink now dried and caked to uselessness.

Waddell leaned back, twisted up and lit a cigarette and peered speculatively through the pale smoke. According to Tim Roach, Frank Scorbie intended to be gone ten days or thereabouts. Why, and where to? Neither by attitude or words had Roach even hinted that this sort of thing was something Scorbie did regularly, or, for that matter, had ever done before. So—why now?

He was still turning this question over in his mind without coming up with any good answer, when Jack Millerson turned in through the door. The store owner was brusk.

'Been doing a little checking up,' he answered bluntly. 'You're right. There's a hole in my business somewhere that's leaking money.'

'So-o?' murmured Waddell.

'Yes,' said Millerson. 'I'm noway sure how much has leaked, but I've done enough general figuring to be sure some has. My books, I know, are right. Norma Vespasian handles them, and that girl doesn't make mistakes.'

'Me,' said Waddell slowly, 'I don't know much of anything about how to run a store. But in your place I'd keep an eye on the cash

172

drawer.'

'My own thought,' growled Millerson. He took a turn up and down the room. 'Damn it, Waddell, I'm going to have to close in on somebody I've trusted. And it isn't a pleasant thing to consider.'

'I can see where it wouldn't be,' Waddell agreed.

'I'm going to make certain—dead certain before I act.'

'Of course,' Waddell nodded.

Millerson paused in his pacing, his back to Waddell while he stared for a moment through the open door. Presently he tipped a fatalistic shoulder and turned.

'I owe you thanks for waking me up. It's so damned easy to drift into a groove of living by habit, and be blind to the things right in front of you. By the way, a pair of boots that Frank Scorbie had me order for him a couple of months ago, came in on this morning's stage. Where is he?'

'That's something I'd like to know, myself,' stated Waddell. 'For I understand he rented a horse from Tim Roach and left town for a few days. Would you have any idea where he went, or why?'

'Not the slightest,' Millerson declared. 'I just asked for him myself, didn't I? No, there was a time when I figured I should have some say in how this camp and its affairs were run. But I soon found myself way outnumbered,

173

with few of the worthwhile people seeming to give a damn, one way or another. So I decided—to hell with it! Anyway, I'm a storekeeper, not a politician.'

'As you see it, who does run Midas Hill?'

Millerson's glance was swift and direct.

'Price Ringgold, mainly. Under him, Hogan Geer handles the Gulch. A time or two I've wondered if Byron Garrison wasn't the quiet man behind the whole setup.'

'That,' observed Waddell, 'would be a pretty complete arrangement, wouldn't it? Pay the miners wages with one hand, take it away from them with the other.'

'It's been done before,' Millerson shrugged. 'Of course you understand that Frank Scorbie takes his orders from Ringgold and Geer; when they snap their fingers he barks and rolls over.'

'I know,' Waddell acknowledged.

'But you don't?'

'No!' curtly—'I don't!'

'Which, in all honesty, Waddell, I've got to wonder about. Why Scorbie keeps you on? Why Ringgold and Geer allow him to keep you on?'

'Simple,' Waddell drawled. 'I just refuse to be fired.'

Millerson stared. 'I will be damned! So that's it, eh? Good man!' He moved on out into the street. A moment later he put his head in the door. 'You ever want a reference,' he called, 'send them to me.'

Waddell stubbed out his cigarette and built another one. Over this one he again frowned troubled thoughts. But presently he dismissed these and got to his feet. For it was past midday and hunger was stirring in him. In the office door he paused, his glance reaching down street where Norma Vespasian crossed through the last few yards to the door of Millerson's store.

She had changed from riding clothes to a simple dress of dark blue, over which was a jacket of cream colored buckskin, into the pockets of which her hands thrust deeply as she strode briskly along. She was an erect girl with prideful shoulders, and she had the trick of carrying her chin slightly tipped, as though in fair challenge to the world.

Waddell smiled musingly, recalling the miles he had ridden with her this day. Good miles, during which she had shown him a brave and cheerful spirit, womanly warmth and understanding, and an honesty so direct it inclined a man to humbleness. He had, Waddell decided, never known anyone quite like her, and in him a long laid away idealism which he had thought completely dead, stirred anew and lifted its head.

He watched until she entered the store, after which he crossed the street to Frenchy's hashhouse. Here was a single diner, lingering over a cup of coffee and a cigar. Ace

MacSwain smiled and tipped his cigar in greeting.

'My friend, it would seem we keep approximate hours. Though this is about as late a breakfast as I've eaten in years.'

'Breakfast? Man alive—you are late!' Waddell took seat beside the gambler. 'I've had a good day of it already. Hired me a horse and rode well away from this damn camp for a while.' He looked at Frenchy Brovarde, who had come along behind the counter. 'Before I order, there's a question or two. Was Frank Scorbie in here this morning?'

Frenchy, swarthy and taciturn, nodded. 'He was here.'

'Did he do any talking or say anything about leaving town for a while?'

'He did not talk.'

'Did you notice where he went after he left here?'

Frenchy shrugged 'He went back to his office. Pretty soon Buff Spooner came out of the office and went away. A little later Scorbie came out and went somewhere up Ute Street. That's all I know. I did not see him again.'

'Thanks,' Waddell said, and gave his order.

Frenchy got busy at his stove. At Waddell's side, Ace MacSwain held his tone to a murmur.

'If I may say so, I had not thought the movements of such as Frank Scorbie to be of much concern to anyone. For, from all I've

176

heard, he's hardly held in what might be called high esteem or respect.'

'In general, you're right,' Waddell admitted grimly. 'And if I was sure his actions were entirely his own, I'd not give them a second thought. What does concern me is what he does or may do on orders from somebody else. In the kind of game I'm in, Ace, you come to learn there's always a good reason behind every move that may come out of the politics of a Ute Street. And if you're reasonably intelligent you guide yourself accordingly. You take nothing for granted. That way you live a little longer.'

'Then Scorbie has done something today on orders from Ute Street?'

'After what Frenchy just told me, I'm certain of it.'

'What did Scorbie do?'

'He left town for a few days.'

Ace MacSwain considered this through several long pulls at his cigar. He shook his head.

'I may be a bit thick today, but I fail to see any particular significance in that.'

'Look at it this way,' explained Waddell. 'Regardless of what he may seem to be now, there was a time when Frank Scorbie was a mighty good man of the law, and a man does not easily shed all of the past good memories of his life. Part of what he once stood for is bound to be with him yet. So, even with one

177

sunk as far in a whiskey bottle as Frank Scorbie seems to be, who knows when some particular happening or condition of affairs may find him standing straight up again, stung with the old pride?'

Again Ace MacSwain considered, to presently nod. 'I can see how that might be. You're suggesting that the powers along Ute Street, fearing just such a possible regeneration over some incident, want him out of the picture for a while?'

'That's right.'

'But they do not want to be rid of him for good?'

'Not for good. Because it is to the advantage of Ute Street to operate behind some semblance of law, preferably the kind that can be managed. So far, Frank Scorbie has been that kind of law.'

'What sort of an occasion could they fear might set him off?'

'This could be entirely wishful thinking on my part,' Waddell said slowly, 'but there was a time when Frank Scorbie and I walked shoulder to shoulder along some damn tough streets. When that sort of thing takes place it can create a bond not easily forgotten.'

'You think Ute Street could have reasoned it so?'

'Hogan Geer might have. The man's a wolf, and a shrewd one.'

'All of which,' observed MacSwain, 'suggests

some move by Ute Street against you.'

Waddell shrugged. 'Weren't odds being laid on how long I'd be around?'

'Just so,' murmured MacSwain. He frowned. 'You cause me worry. I shall make the late round with you again tonight.'

'Thereby, as I have said before, guaranteeing you no friends on Ute Street,' Waddell warned.

'While as I said before, on Ute Street I want no friends,' retorted the gambler. 'About midnight I'll be looking for you at the Palace.'

Frenchy Brovarde came away from his stove to slide Waddell's order across the counter. Eyeing the size of it, Ace MacSwain chuckled.

'Yours must be a strictly clear conscience. Because a guilty one could never live with such a meal.'

'I'm making up for a lot of meals I've missed,' Waddell defended.

MacSwain chuckled again, paid his score and sauntered out.

Later, full fed, Waddell started for his room with the idea of catching a little rest against the long drag of the night hours to come. But crossing the interval beyond the Hill House alley, he recalled something that had been on his mind, earlier. So instead of going straight to the Crowder home he cut over to Vespasian cottage and to the small shed and stable in back of it.

Sound of his approach brought a soft,

equine whicker, which greeted him again with increasing eagerness as he stepped into the stable. Past the gate of a box stall the head of a bay filly lifted and a velvety nose reached toward his outstretched hand. This was the pretty little animal Norma Vespasian had ridden. Moving into the stall, Waddell ran a hand along the animal's back and found it rough with dried sweat. This was as he expected it would be, for late for work on her return to town, Norma had had no time to do more than unsaddle the filly and pull down a feed of wild timothy for it.

Waddell located a curry comb and brush and began giving the filly a grooming. He found a thorough pleasure and satisfaction in the chore. Also in the drowsy gloom and peace of the stable so deep that the buzzing of several blue-bottle flies carried clearly down from among the rafters, along with the rustling of mice in the small hay loft, and with their minute squeaking. Then there was the friendly nuzzling of the filly and the feel of sweat harshened hide turning smooth and silky under his ministrations.

He thought again of the girl who had ridden this horse, how she had looked in the saddle, how quick and fine her laughter, and the full richness of character she had revealed, once ease and understanding had swept aside barriers of earlier doubt.

Also he thought of past years and of the

remoteness of mind and spirit they had somehow armored him with and which he now found so difficult to put aside. This, it seemed, was what the wearing of a law badge could do to a man; make him stand in loneliness, way off by himself. Was that all be wanted of the future, more of that isolation, that loneliness? To stand forever apart, to walk alone, and, some dark and treacherous night, or bright and betraying days, die alone?

He shook his head and swung restless shoulders against the confusion and nagging doubt of his thoughts. Then turned quickly in response to the slightly mocking words which reached him.

'Changed jobs, maybe? Now a stable roustabout?'

Past the gate of the box stall he looked at Lucy Garrison standing in the stable entrance, a shoulder point hooked negligently against the door post. With her back to the light he could make nothing of her expression beyond the faintly jeering twist of her lips.

He rapped the curry comb on the wall of the stall, clearing it.

'A roustabout for a quiet hour,' he admitted briefly. 'And thinking how damned honest and secure a stable can be. How did you get here?'

'I'd been visiting with Mrs. Crowder. I saw you go in here, so I came over.'

'Why?'

She did not answer for a moment, and when

she did her voice was low and without any trace of jeering.

'I'm not sure. Impulse, maybe. Or curiosity. You should feel flattered, Mister Chris Waddell. For I am not in the habit of trailing after men, either on impulse or for any other reason.'

He put curry comb and brush aside, moved from the stall to stand beside her. He got out his tobacco and rolled a cigarette.

'Just what do you expect of me?'

She squared around and looked up at him, and the light, striking in from the side, cut her features into a pattern of highlight and shadow.

'I don't know,' she said, a trifle somberly. 'I really don't know. Maybe if you'll talk with me. Yes, I think that's it. Just talk to me.'

'About—what?'

'Most anything. Except mines and ore and assays—and Garrison respectability!' She ended a trifle fiercely.

'There's nothing wrong with mines, or respectability,' Waddell reminded. Smiling a trifle, he added, 'Though right now the last is getting quite a going over. For you shouldn't seek out strange men in stables, you know— not for any reason.'

She was, he thought, like a pretty child, spoiled and bored.

'I'd make friends with a wooden Indian,' she declared, 'just so I had somebody different to talk to. Dad and his mines. Aunt Clara and her everlasting respectability!'

'Surely your home can't always be as empty as that,' Waddell said. 'Your father—your aunt—they must have friends?'

'Dad, yes. But they all talk of the same things he does. And so far, Aunt Clara hasn't found anyone in Midas Hill who measures up to her idea of Garrison respectability. Of course she'll have no truck with the common herd.'

Waddell showed open amusement. 'What would she think if she saw you here, talking to me?'

'That I was headed straight for the hottest corner of the devil's kitchen. Poor Aunt Clara. She just can't get rid of her conviction that all men are monsters. That is—all but one.'

'And who would that preferred individual be?'

'Price Ringgold.'

'Price Ringgold!' Waddell sobered. 'Your friend, too?'

'No. I hate him!' It was a flat, definite statement. 'He's a cold snake. I don't see how Dad and Aunt Clara can stand him around. And he hates you, you know.'

'I would guess that he might,' Waddell acknowledged. 'How did you learn of it?'

'I heard him ranting to Dad about you, saying you should be run out of camp. I've wondered what you did to him.'

'Mainly refuse to get off the earth when he came by.'

She nodded. 'That would do it. He can't stand to be opposed.' Abruptly she changed the subject. 'How long have you known Norma Vespasian?'

Waddell replied warily. 'Only since I came to Midas Hill.'

'You like her, don't you? Else you wouldn't be caring for her horse.'

'She's a very admirable person,' Waddell said carefully.

'Do you say that about all women?'

'I don't know many women,' fenced Waddell.

'Could you say it about me—and mean it?'

'I could—and I do.'

She studied him for a grave moment. 'Yes,' she nodded, 'you really mean it. But in a strictly impersonal way. For you are a long way off—a very long way—all by yourself. On a high hill, too steep for anyone else to climb.'

'You are shrewder than you appear,' Waddell observed. 'The things you speak of are a penalty of the trade.'

She moved out of the stable door into the slanting afternoon sunshine, speaking in an absent way, as though she might be uttering her thoughts aloud.

'I've been curious from the first and I had to find out. Now I understand.' She turned and looked at him. 'I'm rather sorry for you, Chris

Waddell. Because it must be very, very lonely, up on that hill.'

He stood, puzzled, unable to think of an answer. And she went away, to disappear beyond the Crowder cottage.

Behind him the filly nickered again, greedy for more attention. Waddell crushed the stub of his cigarette against the door post and returned to his grooming chore.

CHAPTER ELEVEN

It was nearing sundown when Buff, youngest of the three Spooner brothers, entered Jack Millerson's store. Just inside the door he paused, looking around. In here the first shadows of approaching sundown were beginning to build. Buff's narrow, animal-wary observation roved the store quickly, coming to rest on Norma Vespasian, where she leaned over some paper work at the far end of the counter. The impact of Buff's fixed stare made her look up. Immediately she knew the feeling of affront.

This was as it had been on several previous occasions when she chanced to find herself under the regard of this lank, dark-faced young Ute Street tough. Always there was an avidness in his glance, a certain air of rapacity to turn her cold, and an insult to outrage her.

So it was now, and though she tried to face him down with cold scorn, she finally had to turn away, her cheeks burning with indignant anger.

Buff Spooner's brief smile was as thinly vicious as a wolf's snarl. In his loutish self-confidence he saw Norma's surging color not as the hot flame of anger and repulsion, but as a self-conscious, coquettish blush. And he made mental note accordingly.

He moved up to the counter and faced Spence Munger across it. He laid down some coins and called for a caddy of Durham tobacco. Then, in lower tone, he made added remark before he took his purchase and went away, moving slowly while he looked again in Norma's direction.

When Buff was finally gone, Spence Munger stood for a considerable interval, staring straight ahead and running the tip of his tongue back and forth across his lips, as if finding them dry and parched.

Buff Spooner turned into Ute Street and there lost himself for a time. But in the first full run of blue sundown shadows he circled above town to come in at the far north corner of the Vespasian cottage, and there set himself to wait.

It was just short of full dark when Norma Vespasian left the store for home and supper. Her mood was a mixed one. Embers of anger over the Buff Spooner incident still smoldered.

Then there was some puzzlement over an abrupt change in manner by Spence Munger. Before Buff Spooner's appearance, Spence had been his usual self about the store, a minor, threadbare personality forever trying by word and attitude to increase his size in the eyes of others. But after Buff Spooner had gone, Spence became a shrunken soul, cloaked by a look of harried worry.

Beyond these things, however, and more than balancing their effect, was the memory of her visit earlier in the day with Chris Waddell. A chance meeting on the Heron Creek trail with a man she had seen before as a distant, reserved, taciturn servant of the law, had evolved into a companionship as thoroughly pleasant as it was surprising.

Equally surprising, now that she considered it, was her own willingness to meet that companionship halfway, and the real pleasure she had found in it.

She thought back to the first time she had seen him, at Decker's Flat, sitting across the supper table from her. A tall, gaunt, almost haggard man who ate with a concentrated restraint even more betraying of his need for food than any open ravening would have been. After which had come the long, all-night ride on Barney Guilfoyle's freight outfit, with this same Chris Waddell a silent, stoic figure beside her on that high, slow-toiling wagon box. At Grizzly Spring he had shown a hint of his

187

real training by his swift, ruthless smashing of the holdup attempt. On arrival at Midas Hill, in succession had come suspicion, resentment and then a grudging concern for this man. Now, finally, there was the start of a friendship which had enabled her to glimpse something of the gentler qualities hidden by the professional cloak of reserved taciturnity. And what she had seen, she had liked.

These were her thoughts as she moved through the alley past the Hill House and across the interval beyond to the modest little dwelling she called home. And as she came up to the door of this, there abruptly beside her, was Buff Spooner. His words struck at her, thin and leering.

'You'll be invitin' me in, of course!'

All her life Norma Vespasian had moved with her father along a rough and ready frontier of mining camps and cattle country, a life that had early taught her a realistic self-reliance. Whenever she rode, a revolver rode with her in one of her saddle bags. But here in town she carried no defensive weapons save native courage and a high pride that could flay and scorn. It did so now.

'Get out of here!' she flared. 'You've no right to even speak to me!'

Not so much the words as the tone. Like the lash of a whip with its scorn and contempt. Buff Spooner reacted to it as he might have to the bite of an actual lash. He snarled and

188

caught at her.

'No you don't! You don't show me the coy and come-on look and then play the proud and haughty lady. I know your kind!'

She tried to fight off his pawing, raking hands, to break by him and get into the house. She had no luck. She could not pull away from him. For the first time in her life she knew a real and frantic fear. It gathered in her throat, swelled and broke from her lips in choked and desperate cry.

Readied for a long night ahead by a couple of hours of sleep and a supper of Mrs. Crowder's best cooking, Chris Waddell had stepped out into the gloom of early dark and paused there to light the smoke he'd just rolled. But even as he would have dragged a match along the leg of his jeans to strike a flame, he froze, high and alert, staring across at the Vespasian cottage. Over there had sounded a woman's cry. Peering through the clotted shadows he made out the struggling bulk of two people. And again came the breathless, straining cry, full of fear and revulsion.

He went across at a run and as he closed in past the corner of the house those struggling figures spun into the clear beside him, then broke apart as Buff Spooner became aware of his presence and dodged aside, cursing his hissing anger. On her part, Norma Vespasian uttered a single word of sobbing relief.

'Chris!'

Charged with black and deadly anger, Waddell drove past her at Buff Spooner, who was now clawing for his gun. Waddell crashed into him, grabbing to smother Buff's draw. There was a wiry, snakelike strength in Buff Spooner, but it was not nearly enough, now.

Waddell tore the gun away from Buff, then threw him back. Buff slammed into the wall of the house and as he bounced off, ran into a fist that had all of Waddell's weight and wild anger behind it. The blow caught Buff in the middle of his face and knocked him headlong. And he got back to his feet only because Waddell hauled him upright before knocking him down again.

Twice more Waddell hauled Buff Spooner upright then smashed him down. Again he lifted his man, but all he held now was a sodden, senseless hulk with dragging legs and feet. Even so, he had his fist drawn back for another blow when Norma Vespasian caught his arm.

'Chris—no! It's all right—now. All right—I tell you!'

Waddell hesitated, every muscle taut and vengeful. Then he loosened his grip and Buff Spooner sprawled limply. Waddell turned.

'How did it happen? Why would such as this fellow be hanging around you?'

The harshness of his tone and words, and what seemed almost like an accusation in

190

them, brought Norma up quiet and steady.

'I know only that when I came home from work, there he was. He grabbed hold of me, and—!'

As abruptly as steadiness had returned, it left again. Her words ran off into a little sob. She pressed her hands to her face, shaking.

Waddell slid an arm about her shoulders and spoke with gruff gentleness. 'Didn't mean that the way it sounded. It's just that the thought of that damned whelp laying hands on you—!'

She rested against him for a moment, then drew away.

'Yes,' she murmured. 'I—I know. Just the thought of that—!'

'You go over and stay with Mrs. Crowder for a while,' Waddell ordered. 'It'll give you a chance to steady down. And here's a promise; this fellow won't be back!'

'What—what are you going to do with him?'

'Run him out of the country.'

But—nothing worse?'

'Not unless he asks for it. That part will depend on him.'

She went away then, to Mrs. Crowder's, and Waddell watched until a flare of lamplight, winking on and off, told of a door that had been opened and closed. After which he turned his attention to the man at his feet, waiting until Buff Spooner began coming out of it, stirring a little, his breathing a stertorous blubbering in a blood-clogged nose and throat.

Waddell collared him and hauled him to his feet, then shoved him along, steering his stumbling, floundering steps over to the alley and through it to Summit Street. Here, in the early flare of light from one of the hotel windows, he stopped and squared his man around.

Buff Spooner showed full effect of the fury that had descended upon him. His face was one great livid, blood-smeared bruise. His lips were puffed, battered and split and seeping blood. One eye was already swollen tightly shut, the other nearly so. His head wobbled loosely as Waddell shook him.

'Take a look at me, Spooner. Take a good look! So you'll know who it was that worked you over. Here is my final word. Come sunrise tomorrow, if you're anywhere in Midas Hill, you'll be dead. Understand me? You'll be—dead!'

Buff Spooner understood. For the first time in his life he had really taken some of the sort of treatment he had many times helped hand out to others. In the space of moments he had been punished fearfully, whipped not only physically, but in spirit as well. Any degree of toughness, real or fancied, that he had possessed before, was not nearly enough to survive what he had taken at the fists of Chris Waddell. In his one eye still capable of some vision, fear lay, naked and dazed.

He tugged weakly against Waddell's grip and Waddell let him go. He lurched off into the gloom, weaving like a drunken man. Waddell watched him out of sight then crossed to the office and stood for a time in front of it while twisting up another smoke and testing the tempo of the night, using this moment to bank and subdue some of the storm of anger still at high heat within him.

A breath of wind flowed down out of the high country, laying the bite of its chill against his cheeks. A pair of ore wagons rumbled past on their way to the corrals at the lower end of Summit. A late arriving stage from Decker's Flat braked to a halt before the Hill House, discharging a cargo of passengers and a mail sack, thereafter also heading for the corrals, making a wheel-skidding turn in the narrow of the street which brought it so close to Waddell he could smell the steamy sweat of the tired team. A little later two riders jogged in from the night, tied in front of Jack Millerson's store and went in there.

A tide of off-shift miners, their day of toil behind them, began to appear. A few moved in at Frenchy's hashhouse and some went as far as Millerson's store. But most made the turn into Ute, and Waddell picked up the quickening growl of that street.

His lips pulled long and thin as he took a final drag at his cigarette then flipped the butt into the dust. Ahead lay a good six hours of nerve-stretching tension through a damned man-made jungle with its furtive shadows, its lust and its wildness and its predatory evil.

Why go on with it? Why not walk away and forget it? What sort of fool was a man to persist in a quixotic purpose that would gain him neither credit nor thanks? Surely a fool, but perhaps a proud one . . . !

He turned into the office and lit the lamp. From the gun rack he lifted down the sawed-off shotgun. He broke the weapon, saw it was empty, then tested the twin locks. On the shelf beside the rack were a couple of boxes of ammunition, one box never opened, the other better than half full. Dusty, faded labels identified the ammunition as being made by the Union Metallic Company, the warranty stating that the loading was three and one half drams of Ffg black powder and twelve pellets of Single O buckshot, and that top performance and reliability in all properly constructed arms was guaranteed.

Waddell slipped two of the shells into the breech of the gun, pocketed half a dozen more, put out the lamp and left the office. He turned into Ute Street, the shotgun cradled across his arm. If the Gulch wanted to make this night a rough one, then rough it would be. Damned rough!

After making his shambling way across Summit into Ute Street, Buff Spooner sought a pocket of darkness, leaned against a wall and was sick, getting rid of the blood that had drained down his throat and which his stomach, in sudden queasiness, now rejected violently. Though walking this far had served to steady him somewhat, it also made him increasingly conscious of his condition. At first a sort of physical numbness had held him, but now this was giving way to pain which slugged his battered face and head with torment. Added to this was the nausea, the sickness. And—the fear!

The fear! The worst of all. A pressure which would not leave him, which moved as he moved and lay on him with smothering weight. During those savage moments when the fury of Chris Waddell had raged, something gave way in the makeup of Buff Spooner; some vital thread which bent and broke and would never be the same again. And now, presently, the fear sent him stumbling along to the retreat of safety which he knew best—the back room of the Belle Union.

He paid no attention to the startled stares which followed him as he made his uncertain way down the length of the barroom; in fact was not even aware of them. Nor did he knock at that rear door, just pushed it wide and lurched through. Under the cone of light above the center table, Hogan Geer and Price Ringgold had their heads together in some kind of conference. Geer came around harshly.

'You know better than to break in here this way. What's the matter with you—you drunk? Get back there and close that door!'

Buff seemed not to hear, just weaved to a chair and fell into it, which brought his face low enough for the light to strike it fully. Geer, about to throw further angry words, held silent for a moment, staring, before snapping another question.

'What in hell happened to you?'

There was no answer. Geer got to his feet, moved to the door and closed it. He came back and stood over Buff.

'You heard me—what happened to you?'

Geer's dominance broke through Buff's mental sluggishness, forcing a single blurted word.

'Waddell.'

'The devil! You mixed with Waddell? Why?'

Buff opened his battered mouth, closed it again. Suddenly he was afraid to voice the real reason. And before Hogan Geer could question him further, the door swung again, letting in his brothers, Elvie and Lee. Geer put his anger on them.

'The three of you have been told a dozen times to knock on that door before you open it. Now you either start obeying orders exactly as I give them, or you're through eating and drinking on me. I can find plenty of others who'll damn well be glad to do as they're told. Now—close—that—door!'

Lee Spooner hastened to obey, while Elvie stared at Buff and spoke sullenly. 'Feller out front said he'd seen Buff come in here and that Buff was hurt. So Lee and me—.'

'He's not hurt bad enough to start any stampede,' Geer cut in acidly. 'Somebody bounced their fists off him, that's all. He claims it was Waddell.'

'Waddell!' Elvie turned toward the door again. 'Anybody hits Buff, hits Lee and me, too. And me and Lee, we'll take care of that feller Waddell right now—once and for all!'

'No you don't!' rapped Geer. 'You go out that door against my orders and you can keep right on traveling. I mean that! You don't come back. I want to know more about this.' He turned to Buff again. 'All right—it was Waddell who worked you over. He must of had a reason. What was it?'

Buff squirmed. He wished now he hadn't come here so directly, but had hid out somewhere else until his mind cleared and he had thought up some reason other than the real one for the beating.

Standing over him, staring down with cold, black eyes, Hogan Geer seemed to read Buff's mind.

'Don't lie to me. I want the truth. Why did Waddell tie into you?'

Buff couldn't face that dark and searching stare. Nor could be any longer evade Geer's bleak demand.

197

'That girl,' he blurted. 'She'd been giving me the eye and when I dropped around to take her up on it, she raised a hell of a row. Next thing I knew, there was Waddell. And—well —!' Buff shrugged.

'So that's it, eh,' said Geer. 'You tried to manhandle a girl. What girl?'

Buff squirmed again before making reluctant admission.

'The one who works for Millerson.'

Hogan Geer jerked forward, grabbing Buff by the shoulder. 'You laid hands on the Vespasian girl? You did? Why you damned stupid lout, do you want to turn the whole camp against us?'

'She gave me the eye,' defended Buff weakly.

'You lie!' snapped Geer. 'That girl's a lady. She wouldn't wipe her feet on the likes of you. It's too bad Waddell didn't break your stupid neck!'

The fear surged up in Buff again as he recalled the import of Chris Waddell's final words.

'Waddell aims to kill me,' he mumbled. 'He said so. Told me if I was in Midas Hill, come tomorrow mornin', I'd be dead. That's what he said.'

Elvie Spooner put his sullen stare on Hogan Geer.

'You see? Well, Lee and me, we ain't waitin' around for this Waddell to come gunnin' for

Buff.'

'You're going to stay right here and do as you're told,' Geer told him. 'I've got my own plans on how to handle Mister Waddell and that's the way it will be.'

Price Ringgold, a silent and sardonic spectator up to now, cleared his throat, waved his cigar and nodded toward Elvie and Lee.

'Maybe you ought to let them go, Geer. After all, you can't expect them to stand by idle while Waddell guns down their brother. And why such concern over the Vespasian girl? Maybe she did give Buff the eye.'

'You know better than that,' Geer said. 'My concern is for the setup we got here and what we can make out of it if we play it smart. Remember what I said before about the law and order spirit? Well, nothing will set off the average man—even if he's a mud-mucking Hunkie in a mine—quicker than mistreatment of a good woman. And every man in this camp who has ever been in Jack Millerson's store and faced Norma Vespasian across the counter, knows she's a damn fine girl. And if any harm should come to her through someone the miners could definitely connect with Ute Street, we could have a mob down on our necks that would tear the whole damn street apart. It's happened in other camps—it can happen here.'

Geer's tone had grown increasingly harsh as he spoke. Now he swung an emphatic hand as he went on.

'I'm getting damn sick and tired trying to talk sense to them who won't listen to it. Maybe, Ringgold, this is a good time to announce that I'm not going to lay my neck on the line for you or Byron Arno Garrison or anybody else unless I have equal voice in how everything is handled. And the part I take in this business is going to be handled the way I think it should be, or I move out. Now, once and for all, what's it going to be?'

For a time it appeared the Spooners were forgotten as Hogan Geer and Price Ringgold locked glances and wills. Then Ringgold tipped a shoulder and his pale eyes veiled slightly as he made thin pronouncement.

'Have it your own way. Buff Spooner's your man, not mine.'

'Yes,' said Geer, 'my man. And I'll look after him in my own way.' He turned to Buff and some of the edge went out of his tone. 'The smart thing, Buff, is for you to get out of town for a while. So you're heading for Gold Run to stay with Charley Urbine for a week or so. With you out of sight, Waddell will think he's got us on the run. Which will be his mistake. Well, Elvie?'

Elvie Spooner considered for a moment, then nodded.

'You want it so, Lee and me, we'll string along. Just so Buff don't get no dirty end of it.'

Price Ringgold took another drag at his

cheroot. 'How about that little chore you three were to take care of for me?'

'You mean—the tinhorn?' asked Elvie.

'I mean the tinhorn.'

'Two's plenty for that,' Elvie scoffed. 'Just Lee and me.'

*　　　*　　　*

In the Palace it was a dull evening. Bar trade had been particularly slow. Scotty Deale yawned and wished the poker game yonder would break up, so that he might close for the night and get a little extra sleep. He realized his wish fairly early, for shortly after the hands of the Sessions clock on the bottle shelf marked the hour of eleven, Lamar Hume pushed back his chair and announced his intention.

'That's it, so far as I'm concerned. These cards hold no interest for me. Maybe I've gone a little stale on poker. At any rate I'm through for the night. I hope you gentlemen don't mind?'

Just three of them were at the table. Hume, Ace MacSwain and Byron A. Garrison. To Hume's words, MacSwain nodded.

'Agreeable with me. Every now and then comes a night like this. Perhaps we miss our usual fourth.'

Lamar Hume snorted. 'You mean Ringgold? Probably still sulking over last night. Garrison, you should teach that fellow the rudiments of sportsmanship. He's your man.'

Garrison answered curtly. 'I hired him as my superintendent. As such, he has proven himself able. Beyond that, his personal character foibles do not concern me. A brandy all around? Good!'

They stood at the bar and drank and then Hume and Garrison went out together. Ace MacSwain bought some cigars, selected one, snipped the tip off carefully and lighted up. He looked at Scotty Deale through the smoke and spoke thoughtfully.

'You ever get sick and tired of moving up and down behind the bar, Scotty—pouring drinks, wiping glasses, listening to idle whiskey talk, day and night, months and years without end? For myself there come times when I feel I never want to see another card. Tonight is one of them, for there was no challenge in that session just finished, and without challenge of some sort there's no flavor in any game, including the one of life.'

There was little capacity for imagination in Scotty Deale and even less for philosophizing. Scotty's was a thoroughly grooved and methodical mind.

'Man's got to do somethin' to earn a livin',' he grumbled. 'And I'll take my job any time to one of runnin' a pick and shovel a thousand feet underground like plenty of fellers in this camp have to do. You wouldn't swap places with one of them, would you?'

MacSwain considered for a little time, a musing half smile on his face.

'Now that you push me into a corner on the question, no I wouldn't,' he admitted. 'Being that sort of weak, pusillanimous human . . . But there is one thing we must admit, which is that the fellow with the pick and shovel underground is of far greater importance to the needs of the world than either of us, and at times I find that fact a little disquieting.'

Scottly blinked as he digested this. Then he shrugged and began taking off his apron.

'I don't know nothin' about this bein' important to the world, and I ain't worryin' any about it. All I know right now is that I'm goin' to get a little extra sleep for a change. G'night!'

Ace MacSwain went out and stood under the chill stars, finding comfort in his cigar as he surveyed the dim and virtually empty expanse of Summit Street. He recalled what he had told Chris Waddell earlier in the day. That he would meet him here at the Palace at midnight. Which time was still the best part of an hour away. What to do until then? A walk? The idea appealed and he set off down street, trailing the fragrance of his cigar across his shoulder.

The gambler strode briskly, for the thin, chill mountain air lifted a man and breathed a fine, free vigor into him, expanding his tissues and quickening his blood. Down at this end of town all was gloom. Jack Millerson's big store and warehouse building was thoroughly dark and there was neither light nor sign of activity about the stage and freight corrals save the sleepy stir of the four-footed occupants of the corrals. Freight and ore wagons loomed ponderously and a stage, a mud wagon and several smaller rigs threw their lesser shadows. Odor of the corrals lay rank and heavy in the still air and the drift of MacSwain's cigar reached an equine nostril and brought a low, gusty snort.

Beyond the corrals the road broke away to dip presently into a stand of timber. Ace MacSwain walked as far as the edge of that black barrier and paused there to smoke out his cigar and luxuriate in the peace of the moment.

He was a man who, because of his profession, held himself behind a wall of cynicism, showing the world a look and attitude at considerable variance with his real self. Over a poker table, hard materialism might be his way, but at a moment like this and in these surroundings he turned his feelings free, and knew an inner exultation that inspired, while holding some of the inescapable sadness of loneliness.

He stood still, very still, letting the fine quality of the night wash all through him . . .

When Ace MacSwain walked away down street from the Palace Elvie and Lee Spooner watched from the concealment of the blackness in the alley by the Hill House.

'Where'd he be goin?' Lee mumbled.

'Don't know,' Elvie told him. 'But we're in luck. For the camp's damn empty down that way at this time of night. Come on!'

They followed carefully, slinking shadows slithering through the protection of deeper shadows. They came presently to the corrals and wagon park, and there Elvie pulled to a halt in the shelter of a towering freighter.

'Far enough. He'll be comin' back this way.'

They hunkered down, lean and vicious and intent.

'He'll have a gun, you think?' Lee wondered.

'One of those belly guns, maybe. Won't do him no good. He won't get a chance to use it. Now keep quiet!'

The night, for all its seeming pause, had its own kind of sound and movement. So far distant as to seem just a fragment of a hoarse, heavy echo, the howl of a timber wolf made its brief drift against the silence. An owl, afloat on noiseless wings, dipped suddenly toward the feed stacks beyond the corrals, and then was gone, taking with it the thin squeaking of the luckless rodent that was pierced and dying in its claws. Overhead, one of the countless, cold-burning stars suddenly streaked across night's vast void and plunged into the oblivion of nothingness.

Man, mused Ace MacSwain, was a mote of dust, caught between the power of the earth and the sky, and of no consequence whatever . . .

His cigar smoked out and cold, and midnight nearing, MacSwain headed back up town. He came in past the corrals and through the wagon yard. And from the black shadow of a big freighter, two driving, lunging figures came at him, smashing into him, knocking him back and down.

They were savage, they were quick, they were merciless. MacSwain fought back as best he could, but the advantage of numbers and initial surprise were all against him. Just once did he manage to roll free and land an effective strike, a kick which caught Lee Spooner low in the body and doubled him up for a moment. But it also turned loose all the wildness that was in Lee Spooner, and when his scrambling hand happened to encounter a sizable chunk of rock that had spilled from one of the ore wagons, he used it as a club, hitting out twice with it before catching Ace MacSwain full on the temple with the third try.

With that blow, everything went away from the gambler and he became just a limp, quiescent shadow against the earth's deeper dark. But the rage vomiting out of Lee Spooner, hung on, and so the rock rose and

206

fell, rose and fell . . . rose and fell . . . !

At five minutes to midnight, Chris Waddell came out of Ute Street and angled over to the Palace. He found the place dark and the door locked. He wondered at that and at where Ace MacSwain, who had promised to meet him here, might be. He stood for a little time, surveying the run of the street's dark, then went along to the Hill House for a look at the hotel's porch. Maybe MacSwain had taken one of the chairs and was waiting there for him. But there was no one on the porch.

Waddell went over to the office, lit the lamp and settled down in the chair behind the desk, laying the sawed-off shotgun on the desk in front of him, glad to be rid of the weight of it.

Tonight, Ute Street had shown him its quietest face since he had taken over the patrol. Yet, for all the comparative peace of the night, he was tired, and he wondered at this. It was a sort of drained out feeling that was more of the spirit than the physical. Probably, he mused, the ashes of the wild anger that had burned in him when he worked Buff Spooner over, and of which some spark still remained.

All evening he had carried that anger with him, and it bad in turn kept alive in him a feeling not too far removed from outright cruelty. Ranging Ute Street and measuring it, he would have welcomed cause to turn that cruelty loose. But it seemed as if the Gulch was aware of this and so moved softly and in deference, for a single altercation between a pair of drunks was the only item of excitement the night had held. This pair he had collared, rapped their heads together, and sent them on their different ways.

He built a cigarette and lay back in his chair, waiting. Either, he decided, Ace MacSwain had forgotten their proposed meeting and turned in for the night, or he was still somewhere about town. In which case he would see the office light and show up presently. He would, decided Waddell, wait half an hour on this chance.

Two cigarettes and thirty minutes later he racked the shotgun, put out the light and headed for his room.

CHAPTER TWELVE

Morning sunlight filtered thinly into Charley Urbine's dingy barroom at Gold Run. Occupying a chair in a shadowed corner, Frank Scorbie suffered in tight lipped silence. He had not had a drink of whiskey since arriving at Gold Run. Last night had been one long hell, as he tossed and rolled, and craving for liquor now had his nerves raw and wild.

Not that there was no whiskey to be had. On the contrary there was plenty of it no further away than that short, battered bar yonder, against which the elephantine figure of Charley Urbine now leaned while sipping a drink of his own. A bottle and another glass stood at Urbine's elbow and Scorbie knew it had been placed there to taunt him.

All he had to do to allay at least part of the nerve scalding agony in him was to walk over to that bottle and help himself, and a dozen times it seemed that he must or go wholly to pieces. Yet every time this conviction gripped him, an even stronger one rose in him, a jaw-hardening wave of stubbornness which raised a barrier of will which would not let him pass.

He couldn't understand it. Inwardly, silently, he cursed that barrier, railed at it as if it were a visible, concrete thing. Which did no good at all. For it was stronger than he was and it was stronger than the pull of the whiskey. And it kept him there in his chair, shaking and suffering, and for the first time in months completely, stone-cold sober.

'Anybody,' taunted Charley Urbine, in his wet, breathy way, 'would think that somewhere between here and Midas Hill, you'd taken the pledge. Or that you figured my whiskey was poison. It ain't. It's damn good whiskey.'

Scorbie did not answer and Urbine lifted his glass to measure the contents against the sunlight in the open door, a puzzled scowl furrowing the moon-round fatness of his face. When word had first reached him from Hogan

Geer that Scorbie would be along presently, Geer's instructions had been few and concise.

Keep Scorbie at Gold Run until sent for. Let him have all the whiskey he wants, which will be plenty. And we in Midas Hill will take care of the bill.

Such had been Hogan Geer's instructions. Scorbie had arrived and the whiskey offered. But he wouldn't touch it. Not a single drink. Instead, near a gallon of black coffee had been substituted. So Charley Urbine wondered, and still staring at his half lifted glass, he made further remark.

'You wouldn't be getting ideas would you, Scorbie? About heading back to Midas Hill, maybe? That wouldn't be wise. You don't go anywhere until I say so. Remember that!'

Still Frank Scorbie said nothing, though his thoughts were as wild as his jumping nerves.

Outside sounded the mutter of approaching hoofs. Charley Urbine tipped his head, listening, then moved to the door, the whole building seeming to sag and creak under his ponderous step.

The arriving hoofs slowed to a trampling halt. Urbine called some remark and got a short muffled answer in return. The rider came across the rickety porch and Urbine gave back from the door to let him enter. Frank Scorbie stared.

The new arrival was Buff Spooner, and in the brief glance Scorbie had at him before the

210

shadows of the room blunted things, he marked the brand of savage punishment which Buff's battered face proclaimed. Charley Urbine marked this also, and spoke on it.

'Who hacked you up? I thought all the grizzly bear had left these hills.'

'Funny,' snarled Buff. 'Funny as hell. Only— it ain't!'

A tide of red rolled up Urbine's vast features, and his fat squeezed eyes turned piggy and cold.

'Listen, Spooner,' he wheezed. 'I don't know why you're here and I don't give a damn. But this is my place and I run it my way. In it I take no back talk from you or any other man. I asked you a fair question. I want a fair answer or you can fork that saddle outside and keep travelin'. Well?'

A week ago, Buff Spooner might have thrown the ultimatum back into Urbine's face. But a week ago, Buff Spooner had been a comparatively whole man, such as it was. He wasn't whole any more. Part of him had been forever lost under the punishing fists of Chris Waddell. So now Buff's snarl turned to a surly mumble.

'Waddell,' he blurted. 'That damned drifter who's set himself up as night marshal in Midas Hill. He jumped me when I wasn't lookin'.'

'So-o?' Urbine's murmured word was caustic. 'Well, one thing is plain enough. When he jumped you he sure must have lit all over

211

you. Put the fear of God into you, too, most likely. Else why would you be here instead of staying on in Midas Hill?'

'Hogan Geer figgered I better come here for a week or so.'

'Sure it wasn't this feller Waddell who told you to get out of town?' Urbine persisted. 'I know how men like him work. They ain't chancing such as you hanging around to gulch 'em from an alley some dark night. After cleaning up like he did on you the idea is to lay out a deadline, generally sunrise or sundown. Either way, it's get out or get gunned. Right?'

Buff nodded. 'He said I'd be dead if I wasn't out of Midas Hill by this morning. But it was Geer who sent me here.' Buff eyed the bottle on the bar thirstily. 'That just an ornament?'

Urbine did not answer for a moment. It was the mention of Hogan Geer's name which decided him. Hogan Geer could foot this fellow's liquor bill, too.

'Help yourself.'

Buff wasted no time. He filled the glass, tossed it off, filled it again. Urbine circled heavily around behind the bar and rescued the bottle.

'I ain't never seen this feller Waddell,' he observed. 'But some word about him has been comin' through. Appears he's got a rind on him. Hear he buffaloed Breed Garvey—and good! That right?'

'Yeah, that's right. And ever since he's been

walkin' up and down Ute Street like he owned it. But he won't do that too long,' Buff added viciously. 'Geer and Breed Garvey and Price Ringgold, they're fixin' to take care of Mister Waddell.' He drained his glass a second time and pushed it toward Urbine in broad hint.

The two big shots of liquor were taking hold now, flushing Buff's bruised and beaten face, putting an arrogant swing to his shoulders. Charley Urbine considered a moment then filled the glass for a third time. After which he corked the bottle and put it away under the bar.

'What did Waddell climb your frame about?'

'A girl,' boasted Buff, now full of whiskey truculence. 'One that works in Jack Millerson's store. She gave me the eye and when I went to see her about it, this feller Waddell stepped in. Like I say, he hit me when I wasn't lookin'. That's how he got an edge on me. How are chances for breakfast?'

'Out back,' Urbine said, leading the way.

Buff Spooner put away his third whiskey and followed.

In his shadowy corner, Frank Scorbie sat quietly. At no time had Buff Spooner looked his way, was apparently unaware of his presence. Whiskey hunger was suddenly forgotten. Running through Scorbie's mind and strangely cooling it, was the import of what he had just seen and listened to.

213

Chris—Chris Waddell was walking Ute Street and making it behave. Making such as Geer and Ringgold and Breed Garvey step aside. But they were figuring to get him, and when they did it would be from behind. Or from the dark, when he wasn't looking . . .

In his mind's eye, Scorbie could see Waddell making his rounds, high and spare and hawkish. A proud man, who would never compromise his authority or tarnish his badge. Yeah, Chris Waddell—with whom he himself had once walked just as proudly, intent on the same unwavering duty.

Chris Waddell, who had whipped Buff Spooner down to the craven whelp that he was. And why? Because of some insult Spooner had offered Norma Vespasian, the girl who worked for Jack Millerson.

As he considered this fact, anger blazed in Frank Scorbie, a kind of anger he had not known for a long, long time. Not the weak, blustering, frustrated whiskey anger that had become so much a part of him, but the old clear flame that had carried him through some of the most danger roughened, but best moments of his life.

From the first time he saw her, he had admired Norma Vespasian. Always from a distance, of course, and with full realization that she was as unattainable as a star. Even when passing her on the street and reading cool contempt in her glance, still had h̲

214

admired and held the best of his thoughts for her.

And such scum as Buff Spooner had dared offer her affront!

The clear flame blazed higher, bringing Scorbie to his feet. He climbed the rickety stairway to his barren room. He stowed his frugal gear in his saddle-bags, checked his gun carefully, and returned to the barroom. He settled back in his chair again and waited the reappearance of Charley Urbine and Buff Spooner.

When they showed, Buff Spooner was saying—'Have my horse looked after and show me a place where I can sleep. I had damn little of that, last night.'

Frank Scorbie got to his feet and came forward. His words fell curtly.

'You'll not sleep here, Spooner. When Chris Waddell told you to get out of Midas Hill, he meant clear the country complete. So get on that horse again and keep traveling!'

Buff Spooner stopped in his tracks. 'Be damned! Scorbie! What in hell are you doing here?'

'No concern of yours,' Scorbie told him shortly. 'I've made it plain what you're to do. Keep traveling!'

Buff Spooner squared around, his puffed lips curling.

'Don't tell me you're trying to be a man again and throw your weight around. Don't tell

215

me that, Scorbie. It won't work.'

'Yes,' said Scorbie steadily, 'it will work. On your way!'

Buff Spooner laughed scornfully. 'Why you damned useless drunk!' He spat at Scorbie's feet.

This last was a measure of contempt he'd shown before. And Scorbie hit him across the face, a stiff-fingered, backhanded slap which set Buff on his heels.

Behind the blow lay a man's burning memory of all past indignities and ill-treatment taken at the hands of Buff Spooner and others of his ilk in Midas Hill. Also, it carried Frank Scorbie's championing of a girl who had never spoken to him or offered him any sign of friendship. In effect, it was a blow in defense of an ideal.

It not only set Buff Spooner on his heels, but it started again the burning pain in his bruised and blackened face. Backed by the whiskey he'd taken on, it turned loose a weak rage in Buff. He had a gun tucked under his belt, well to one side where his coat covered it. Now he grabbed for the weapon.

Halfway through the move he grunted and went very still. For the muzzle of Frank Scorbie's gun stabbed him in the belly.

'Go ahead!' invited Scorbie bleakly. 'Throw your gun. See how far you get. Go ahead— throw it!'

Slowly, and with the greatest care, Buff

brought his hand into view. And he brought it empty.

Scorbie's lip curled. 'So! No wolf after all. Just a yellow whelp!'

He reached under Buff's coat with his free hand, took over Buff's weapon, then struck him across the side of the neck with a rigid forearm, sending him staggering.

'That's it,' said Scorbie savagely, 'get away from me. Get a long way away. I told you to haul out of here. I meant it. Get out!'

The shock of that gun muzzle jammed so violently into his belly, and the realization that death had looked at him and breathed coldly upon him, had knocked all the whiskey courage out of Buff Spooner. A trickle of crimson, started afresh by Frank Scorbie's back-hand slap, showed at the corner of Buff's mouth. He licked at it nervously and backed toward the door, Scorbie following him, step by step.

'All right!' Buff mumbled thickly. 'All right—I'll go.'

'And not to Midas Hill, either,' Scorbie warned. 'South is your direction. Don't ever come back!'

Buff did not argue. He climbed into the saddle and went away. To the south.

Frank Scorbie watched him out of sight, then turned to Charley Urbine, terse with an order.

'Have my horse brought around!'

It had for some time been Charley Urbine's fancy that his authority in all things in Gold Run, this furtive ghost of what had once been a boom camp, was close to being absolute. Men came to Gold Run pretty much at his favor and stayed there by the same. And, while he was no coward, neither was he a fool. He had long since learned that it was good sense and good business to read certain signs carefully and then to be guided by them. Within the past few minutes he had read some signs which startled him and made him cautious.

This man who now stood before him was the same one who had ridden in to Gold Run yesterday, a man emerging from a long bout with whiskey; a man shaking, uncertain, dazed and, apparently, one completely whipped by life and circumstance. Yes, this was that same man—but only in the flesh. For the spirit now showing so hard and bright was something else, a flaring renewal of something which could not be guessed at or foreseen. But real— savagely real!

The swiftness of Scorbie's move when he drew on Buff Spooner had not been lost on Urbine, either. Something had amazingly revitalized this man. He was not one to be fooled with and it was plain that any attempt to talk back now would be worse than stupid. And Charley Urbine was not stupid. After all, any debt of friendship he owed Hogan Geer was pretty tenuous, and certainly not of enough account to risk a bullet. Having thus reasoned, he swung his elephantine bulk through the door to the porch and from there raised his breathy yell.

'Spike! Saddle Scorbie's horse and bring it up!'

Ten minutes later Frank Scorbie rode away from Gold Run, and he rode north, toward Midas Hill.

* * *

A knock at the door of his room roused Chris Waddell. He pushed up on one elbow.

'Yes—who is it?'

'Tim Roach,' came the reply. 'Want to see you.'

Waddell blinked, wondering. He called—'Door's unlocked. Come on in.'

Roach did so and without preamble of any sort made his blunt and literal announcement.

'There's a dead man down by my corrals.'

'Dead man?' Waddell threw his blankets aside.

'That's right. Looks like somebody beat him to death with a rock. Being that you pack the law badge, I figgered you'd want to know.'

'Of course,' Waddell said. 'Any idea who it is?'

'It's that gambler who hit town a couple or three days ago. The one that's been playin' in the Palace. Name's MacSwain, I think.'

As he started to pull his shirt on over his head, Chris Waddell's expression had still held some of the relaxation of his interrupted sleep. But now, as he settled the garment fully into place, his look was one of cold bleakness.

'And beat to death with a rock?'

Tim Roach nodded. 'I'd say so from the way things looked. I sent one of my roustabouts after Doc Stone. Doc should be able to tell for sure. All I'm certain of is the man is dead.'

Waddell swiftly finished his dressing, buckled on his gun and led the way out of the house. In the east above the mountain crests the sky was beginning to burn with the promise of sunrise, but here in Midas Hill, morning light held on, gray and dank. The town was not visibly astir yet, but the scent of woodsmoke on the air told of breakfast fires being started here and there.

Down by the corrals, almost under the cold shadow of a towering freight wagon, Doc Stone and a pair of corral roustabouts made a small, crouched group beside a prone figure. As Waddell and Tim Roach arrived, Doc Stone looked up, bristling.

'There are times, by God,' he rumbled, 'when I'm tempted to say to hell with all humans, and never lift a finger again to save the hide of another one of them. Because so damned many are not worth saving. Tell me— just what kind of a two-legged animal would

220

treat a fellow human this way—beat his head in with a rock? Man—who likes to consider himself the highest order of the species! Highest order—hell!'

Chris Waddell looked down at the face of Ace MacSwain and knew an inner sickness. 'About when would you say it happened, Doc?'

'At a guess—around midnight. Whoever did it turned his pockets inside out, too.'

'He put up a good fight,' remarked one of the roustabouts. 'And by the signs, I'd guess that mebbe there was two of them jumped him.'

'I hope he marked them,' ground out Waddell harshly. 'I hope he put a brand on them I can recognize.'

'You knew him pretty well?' Doc asked.

'As well as anybody in Midas Hill. Maybe better than anybody. He was a smart man and a damned good human one. He was my friend. I'm going to keep remembering that.'

'I understand he roomed in the Hill House,' Doc said. 'You'll take over his effects, and if he's got any relatives, get in touch with them?'

'Yes,' promised Waddell, 'I'll do that.'

Doc turned to the roustabouts. 'Let's get this poor devil under cover and out of sight. I'll see to the rest of it.'

'I'd like to pay my share,' Waddell said.

'Let you know if that's necessary,' nodded Doc.

They carried Ace MacSwain into the livery

barn and laid him down on the floor of a harness room. After which Chris Waddell returned to the street and tramped slowly up it, facing the full strike of the sun's first rays. Inwardly he neither saw the sun nor felt its warmth, for his mood was black and somber, and there was no room in him for anything save an edged grief and a seething, wicked anger.

For the first time since coming to Midas Hill he turned through the door of the Hill House. And came face to face with Price Ringgold who was about to leave. Ringgold started slightly and would have passed without a word. But Waddell caught him by the arm and whirled him to a stop.

Ringgold, swiftly furious, tried to jerk away.

'Keep your damned hands off me! Who do you think you are? What's the idea?'

Again he tried to wrench free, and again Waddell whirled him around, this time slamming him against the wall and holding him there with a braced forearm against his chest.

'The idea,' stated Waddell harshly, 'is to get some answers to a couple of questions. Now you can make it easy on yourself, or you can make it rough. But I want those answers. Where were you around twelve, last night?'

'None of your damned business!' spat Ringgold.

Waddell leaned full weight into the pressure

of that braced forearm.

'I'm making it so,' was his cold ultimatum. 'And if you think I'm in a mood to take any more back-talk, you couldn't be worse mistaken. I want an answer and a straight one. Where were you at midnight?'

Caution began to drill through Price Ringgold. Arrogant and self-centered though he was, and fond of nurturing a private sneering scorn of other men, there was still a slyness in him which made him weigh all angles with more than ordinary concern. Also, he was one to put considerable reliance on his instincts, which just now were warning him to go easy with his show of truculent indignation. In consequence, he modified both tone and attitude.

'If you must know, I was in my room, sound asleep.'

'You can prove that?'

'I can prove it. I turned in early, last night. About ten o'clock. Ask Bert Leeds, yonder at the desk. He saw me go up. Now that's out of the way, maybe I've the right to know what this is all about?'

'It's about what happened last night,' Waddell said flatly. 'Somewhere around midnight, Ace MacSwain was killed: beat to death with a rock. Also, his pockets were cleaned. Now this I know. Since arriving in Midas Hill he won a pretty considerable amount from you over Scotty Deale's poker table, a fact which plainly hasn't set well with you. I know, too, that you're more than passably well known in some of the toughest deadfalls on Ute Street. Yes, you're well acquainted along the Gulch. So, everything considered, it's not too hard to suspect possible motive on your part—even some degree of hand in the killing. Well?'

Speaking, Waddell held Ringgold with a steady stare, searching for betraying reaction. He saw immediately he'd gain nothing here. For there was no mistaking the very real flare of surprise that showed in Ringgold's pale eyes. Genuine as this expression was, it was visible for a moment only, then was masked by a hardness which hid everything as effectively as if a door had been tightly closed.

'News to me,' Ringgold said. 'I don't run around hitting people on the head with rocks. You got a hell of a gall, making loose accusations like that.'

'Whatever I have to do to get at the truth, that I'll do,' was Waddell's grim reply.

He loosed his hold and stepped back. Ringgold shrugged his coat to smoothness across his shoulders, felt of his collar, his string tie and straightened the hat on his tawny head. There was a sort of feline fastidiousness about him. His glance was pale and baleful and a touch of the former truculence returned to his tone.

'Now if you're quite sure there's nothing

else—?'

'Not now,' said Waddell curtly. 'But you damn well better hope I don't find out something, later on.'

Ringgold stepped into the doorway, paused there as if to make some retort, but held it back under the impact of Waddell's remorseless, challenging stare. He turned quickly and went away.

Waddell moved over to the desk at the far side of the hotel lobby, where Bert Leeds, a colorless, dry-cheeked man stood, still wide-eyed and startled at what he had heard and observed passing between Waddell and Price Ringgold. Waddell wasted no time on useless preliminaries.

'You heard the question I asked that fellow, and you heard his answer. Was he telling the truth about being in his room at midnight?'

Leeds nodded, swallowing nervously. 'Yes. He did come in early. Around ten, it was. I was here all evening. He did not go out again. What you said—about Mr. MacSwain—there is no mistake?'

'No mistake. What room did MacSwain have. I want to look after his effects.'

'Room Five. I'll go up with you.'

'No!' corrected Waddell. 'That's not necessary. I'll handle matters alone.'

The room was neatly plain. The bed had not been slept in. The only luggage was a small gripsack. It held little in the way of

225

possessions. A razor, a comb and brush, a few items of spare clothing and five gold double eagles in a little buckskin pouch. Plainly, Ace MacSwain was one who preferred to travel light, and whatever his past and his connections, to leave them thoroughly behind.

Waddell had spread the contents on the bed. Now he replaced them, and carrying the gripsack, returned downstairs to the lobby. Bert Leeds was still at the desk.

'Did MacSwain owe you anything for lodging?' Waddell asked.

Leeds shook his head. 'He paid for his room in advance up to the first of the month. I'll be glad to refund the money.'

'Keep it,' Waddell said. 'It could do him no good, and there is nothing in his effects to show that he has any relatives. Did he ever receive or send out any mail that you know of?'

Leeds shook his head again, speaking with real regret.

'It grieves me, this word on Mr. MacSwain. He was a gentleman. I liked him.'

'That,' said Waddell, 'makes two of us.'

He went out, pausing on the hotel porch as a whiff of savory breakfast cooking reached him from Frenchy's. You couldn't, he mused bitterly, drive a sure, direct way to the answers he wanted. And going hungry wouldn't sharpen his own mind any.

By the time he had eaten and returned to

226

the street, town was astir to the new day. Jack Millerson's store was open and old Dad Weyl was sweeping the porch of it. Upstreet at the Palace, the doors were also wide and Scotty Deale was industrious there with a broom. He paused in his labors as Waddell strode up.

'Every time it's a new day and I see you still around, I got to wonder about it,' Scotty remarked. 'You're tougher than I thought.' Shrewdly he added, 'Right now, though, there's a damn dark look to you.'

'The news,' said Waddell succinctly, 'isn't good. You haven't heard about Ace MacSwain?'

Scotty straightened, leaned on his broom. 'No. What about him?'

Waddell told him, and in turn shock, then slow anger swept across Scotty's face. Scotty Deale was a thoroughly practical soul, with little gift of sentiment. But he shook his head gloomily, now.

'This hurts me. I liked the man. He was all right.'

'What time did he leave here last night?' Waddell asked.

Scotty considered a moment. 'Some earlier than usual. Business was slow all around and only Ace and Hume and Garrison sat in on the usual game. Ringgold never showed. The poker game broke up early, right after eleven. So I closed up. That was when MacSwain left.'

'Nobody else was around?' Waddell probed.

'Nobody,' Scotty said. 'You got any lead on who might have done it?'

'Not yet,' Waddell admitted. 'But I'm hoping.'

From the Palace he tramped over to the office, cloaked in his troubled thoughts. He put Ace MacSwain's gripsack on the desk and was settling back for a cigarette and further thought, when a light step at the door brought him to his feet to face Norma Vespasian. She looked her usual crisp and vital self, but her eyes carried a sober concern. She made simple and direct announcement.

'I was on my way to work and I saw you cross the street, and something told me you were carrying an extra load of trouble. What is it, Chris? The Spooners again? I wouldn't want them out after you because of me—of that—that affair last evening when—when—' She flushed and her words ran out.

'No part of that at all,' he assured her quickly. 'This s something else entirely. I dislike spoiling your morning, but may as well tell you, for the word is bound to get around. A man was killed last night, and robbed. A good man. A friend of mine. Ace MacSwain, a gambler, but a square one. He was beat to death and his pockets looted.'

Norma's eyes widened. 'How awful! Ute Street, you think?'

He nodded. 'Ute Street, most probably.'

'And so you'll comb it from end to end?'

228

'How did you guess?'

'It's the kind of person you are,' she proclaimed simply. 'And the fact concerns and frightens me.'

'Why should it?'

She faced him squarely, her chin up, her cheeks warm with quick color. 'Under the circumstances, that question isn't a fair one,' she told him.

The harshness faded from Waddell's face.

'Under the circumstances,' he said gently, 'I withdraw it. And I want to state that by coming here, speaking to me and letting me look at you, you've saved the morning for me.'

Behind his words was far deeper meaning than they appeared to convey, and this she understood. So now, despite the pressure of somber events all about them, these two deeply responsive people were caught up by a current of feeling that lifted them and quickened them and held them almost breathless through a long moment.

It was Norma who ended that moment by moving toward the door. 'You will go your own way of course,' she said, her voice a trifle unsteady, 'and you will live up to your own professional code. I would not stop you if I could—but, oh Chris—you'll be careful?'

A smile touched his lips. 'And is that a fair question?'

'Yes,' she said, 'it is—under the circumstances.'

'Well then,' he said, 'I'll be careful.'

CHAPTER THIRTEEN

The Belle Union, built against the east slope of the Gulch, seemed on casual appraisal to be just a one-story building. Actually, at the rear, due to the slope, there was a sort of step-up addition which was Hogan Geer's living quarters. Here he slept, here he cooked and ate most of his meals. And here Price Ringgold found him, stirring up the fire, preparatory to getting breakfast.

Geer was shuffling around in his undershirt, trousers sagging at his hips, suspenders looped and flopping. With his naked, bony head, his narrow, hooked features and skinny, protruding shoulder blades, he was remindful of a bird of carrion or of prey, hunched against morning's cold. If he was surprised at Ringgold's entrance, he hid the fact well behind an expression of morning sourness.

'What you after,' he demanded, 'breakfast?'

The room was dull with dingy light and full of stale sleeping odors. Ringgold made no effort to hide a grimace of distaste. He gave out a question of his own.

'You hear about that tinhorn, MacSwain?'

Geer, fussing with a coffee pot on the stove, came around.

230

'What about him?'

'He's dead. Beat to death. Those damn fool Spooners—!'

A glint of surprise showed in Geer's eyes. 'Dead, eh?' He considered this far a moment, then added callously, 'Well that's what you wanted, wasn't it? Seems I recall you told the boys to get rid of him.'

'I never said to kill him. I said to run him out of Midas Hill.'

Geer shrugged. 'There's some who won't run. Some you got to handle rougher. Well, you asked Elvie and Lee to do a job for you and they did. That's the all of it.'

'No,' differed Ringgold, 'it's not all. That fellow Waddell is on the prod and there could be hell to pay. I met up with him at the Hill House and he's got the look about him. Somebody's going to get hurt over this—hurt bad! Those Spooners—those damned ignorant thugs—!'

Ringgold took a turn up and down the room, driven by his agitation.

'What's Waddell know about it?' Geer asked. 'Outside of the tinhorn being dead? He don't know who did it and he can't prove a thing.'

'Maybe—maybe!' Ringgold exclaimed irritably, 'but right now he's guessing damn close.'

Geer's black eyes showed a narrowing shrewdness. 'He must have said things to you?'

'He said plenty! You've made a lot of talk about not stirring up the law and order urge in this camp. Well, it could be stirred up now—and good!'

Geer shrugged again. 'Not necessarily. What if Waddell is on the prowl. He's just one man and will be taken care of. The camp itself isn't going to get worked up over the tinhorn. Nobody gives a damn about a tinhorn.'

Ringgold wasn't mollified. 'A tinhorn manhandled, but still live is one thing. A tinhorn dead is something else. Especially the way MacSwain was killed. They beat him to death with a rock.'

'So what?' grunted Geer sarcastically. 'A rock, a club a gun barrel—what's the difference, so long as a job is done?'

'But I didn't want them to go that far,' Ringgold protested. 'What I wanted of them was to handle MacSwain like they did Rufe Belsen when they ran him out of camp. That would have been plenty.'

Geer turned back to the stove, spooned coffee into the pot. 'Like I said, some will run, some won't. Belsen was one kind. The tinhorn was another.'

'MacSwain wasn't given a chance to run,' Ringgold insisted moodily. He added something he'd said before. 'The Spooners—those damn ignorant thugs—!'

Hogan Geer, abruptly out of patience, came around again.

232

'Quit your damn whining. I'm sick of it. This Waddell, he's got you scared to death. Now maybe Elvie and Lee did go some further than necessary in how they handled the tinhorn, but by God, you were the one who sicced them on him. So don't try and crawl from under and lay all the blame on them. You're up to your neck in everything this street stands for, just the same as me or Breed Garvey or the Spooner boys or anybody else. While everything ran along smooth and fat, you were more than glad to grab on to your share of the take. Now that things have roughened up some, because Waddell has moved into the picture, don't think you can slide out a side door and leave the rest of us hanging. You ride just as high as we do, or you fall just as far.'

'I'm not trying to slide out of anything,' Ringgold retorted. 'I'm just deploring what wasn't necessary.'

'Deplore and be damned!' Geer snapped, the well of venom in him still stirred up. 'The cold fact is, you asked Elvie and Lee to take care of the tinhorn. Which they did. And if Waddell should be looking your way and wondering, you'll just have to stand up to it. Just don't try and crawl out. You do, you'll never make it!'

The coffee pot had begun to steam and turn over and Geer took it off the heat and settled the grounds with a dash of cold water. After which he selected a cup of heavy china and

233

poured it full. He nursed this in both hands and sipped at it greedily. 'You want some,' he said between gulps, 'help yourself.'

Price Ringgold had little appetite for coffee or anything else just now. Particularly in this place. But the instincts he trusted warned him to accept, so be selected the cleaner of the two remaining cups and poured a couple of swallows into it.

The coffee seemed to mellow Hogan Geer somewhat.

'You can quit worrying about Waddell. He'll be taken care of. It's all settled.'

'Who ever goes after him better be good,' Ringgold warned. 'Because I got a feeling about that fellow.'

'They'll be good enough,' Geer said. 'Now this tinhorn affair is over and done with. Nobody but us knows for sure who did it. And from now on, we don't know anything about it, either. Understand? We don't know a thing!'

Over on Summit Street, Tim Roach, for the second time this morning, sought Chris Waddell and found him still in the office, bitter-tongued from several successive cigarettes and darkly brooding in his search for some certain answer to Ace MacSwain's brutal death. As was his direct, blunt way, the corral owner wasted no time in coming to the point.

'Took another look at where the ruckus happened, and come up with this. It was most hidden in the dust, but I happened to catch

234

sight of it. Figgered you'd be interested.'

The object he laid on the desk in front of Waddell was a silver dollar. It had been long carried by someone, for it was badly worn and the date, 1884, was barely discernible. It was still round but not truly flat, being cupped and twisted, as if at one time it had been struck a violent blow. Close to the edge, above the profile, a small hole had been drilled, and even the rim of this showed wear.

'What d'you make of it?' Roach asked, after Waddell had examined the coin.

'Looks like somebody's luck piece,' Waddell decided. 'It could have been lost by MacSwain, or whoever was in on the beating. Or it could have been lost some time ago.'

'You look careful,' said Roach, 'you see where it looks like it might have been linked on to somethin'—say a watch chain. And by all the signs, the gamblin' feller put up a real fight. Easy for that dollar to tear loose at a time like that.'

'Yes,' murmured Waddell. 'Yes. I don't recall seeing anything of the sort on MacSwain. But somebody in this camp might have seen it before on someone, which could give me a lead. Tim, you'll say nothing about it to anyone until I've had a chance to run it down?'

'I'll say nothing,' Roach promised. 'I've been around camps like this all my life, and if I've learned one thing, it's that a man's health stays better if he's learned the good lesson of keeping his mouth shut.'

The corral owner turned to the door, hesitated, went out. And almost immediately came back in again, to face Waddell half defiantly.

'It's no use,' he said gruffly. 'You don't need to look no further than me to find out who that luck piece belongs to. I know. Now keepin' a shut mouth may be the mark of a smart man, but there's times when it can also make him a damn coward in his own view, which can be a ranklin' thing that will keep him from sleepin' sound of nights. And any time a man, because he's despising himself, can no longer rest easy in his own bed, then he's better off dead. Yeah, I know who's the owner of that. I've seen him wearin' it. I heard tell he kept it because it once saved his life, glancin' off a bullet to just scar his ribs instead of diggin' plumb into him, like was intended. The dollar belongs to Elvie Spooner!'

'Ah!' exclaimed Waddell softly. 'That does it, Tim. You're a damned good man!'

'I'm a damned, mouthy old fool,' Roach growled. 'With no sense at all. But it was a wicked thing they did to the gamblin' feller, and I just couldn't swallow it without chokin'. When you go after them Spooners—good luck to you!'

Again Tim Roach left, and this time he kept going.

236

Chris Waddell got to his feet and stood for some time, staring down at the battered coin. The settled anger in him was quickening, and with it grew a fine, singing thread of alertness. These two, he knew, from former experience, would presently combine into a cold purpose which would carry him the length and breadth of Ute Street and through every dive and deadfall and dark noisome corner until he came up with those he sought. After that—?

Elvie Spooner's luck piece, eh? Well, there were two kinds of luck, and this time Elvie had used up all his good kind. Sign at the scene of the attack had indicated at least two took part. Which figured. Elvie and Lee Spooner.

Buff Spooner, what about him? In the turmoil of the morning he had not thought of Buff. He did so now, recalling the ultimatum he had laid down to Buff last night. Be out of Midas Hill by sunup this day—or never leave it! Had Buff followed orders? If not, wherever he found Elvie and Lee, there also would he find Buff. Which meant the odds would be heavy.

Well, he had looked at heavy odds before and handled them. For one thing, there was the power of the badge on his side, carrying the weight of an authority that always gave an edge to the man wearing it. Then there was that shotgun on the rack yonder. And finally, there was the certainty of purpose with which he would move, against the uncertainty of the guilty.

These were things experience had taught him, and these were the things he would be armed with when he walked down Ute Street. He put the betraying coin in his pocket and went over to the gun rack. He was about to lift down the shotgun when old Dad Weyl filled the office doorway. As Tim Roach had done, old Dad came directly to the point.

'Mr. Millerson would like to see you at the store, Marshal. Right away. It—it's important. Spence—Spence Munger—he's gone all to pieces. He's talking and saying all manner of the wildest things—!'

'Such as—?' Waddell prompted.

'Well, for one thing that he and somebody named Melton were going to kill you. At least they'd been ordered to. But Spence—he's gone to pieces—and he's talking.'

'Let's get down there,' said Waddell curtly.

When they reached the store the door was closed and locked, but at Dad Weyl's knock, Jack Millerson let them in, then locked the door behind them again. Grimly he said:

'We want no outsiders in on the washing of our dirty clothes.' He jerked a nod. 'Back yonder.'

At the far end of the counter, Spence Munger was hunched on a nail keg, his hands clenched between his knees in an effort to keep them from shaking, his head tipped forward as he stared blindly at the floor.

Beyond him, erect and still, Norma Vespasian stood. And as Waddell met her eyes, he saw in them pity, and a quiet pleading.

Jack Millerson gruffly cleared his throat.

'All right, Spence. Here's Marshal Waddell. Tell him what you've told us.'

For one swift glance at Waddell, Spence Munger tipped up a white and fear pinched face, then dropped back into his original position, lips working without sound, his Adam's apple running up and down a dry, taut throat. Waddell put a hand on his shoulder and spoke, not unkindly.

'Tell it, Spence.'

Spence gulped and gulped again. Then the words came in a rush, jumbled and almost incoherent. From them Waddell got the gist of a sordid picture.

Spence had tried to buck the tiger in Breed Garvey's deadfall. He had lost. Trying to recoup he had on several occasions taken money from the store cash drawer. This he lost, too. Desperate, he had plunged more heavily, signing several I.O.Us. It was the old, old story. The more he tried to get out of the mire, the deeper he sank and the tighter it closed about him.

Using the I.O.Us as a club, Garvey threatened all manner of things. But one day he offered to tear them up if Spence would get him information on when Jack Millerson would next be bringing in some specie from the Spanish Junction bank, and by what means and route. In his fear and desperation, this Spence had done, and Garvey had sent a certain saddle drifter who hung around the Staghorn, one Rube Kelton, out to make a holdup at Grizzly Spring. But the holdup hadn't panned out and Kelton got back to town with a bullet hole in his arm.

Now came the bitter blow. When Spence demanded the I.O.Us, Garvey refused to hand them over, saying that as long as the first attempt at Millerson's specie hadn't panned out, he'd hold them until Spence brought him information about the next specie shipment. All of which, gulped Spence, was bad enough. But it wasn't the worst.

By Buff Spooner, Hogan Geer had sent word he wanted to see Spence at the Belle Union. When Spence managed to slip down there, he found Breed Garvey waiting with Geer. They told him they had something else for him to do, and that if he didn't go along with them, they'd see that word of his part in the first specie deal would reach the ears of Jack Millerson, and that he, Spence Munger, would then be in for long years behind the bars of the territorial prison at Deer Foot.

Stunned by mere thought of this possibility, Spence paused in his outpouring, and Waddell prompted him quietly.

'The something else you were to do was kill me, wasn't it, Spencer?'

240

Spence gulped again, clasped his shaking hands tighter, nodding.

'And this fellow Kelton was to help you?'

'He—he was going to back me up,' Spence mumbled. 'In case I missed you.'

'When and where was it to happen, Spence?' Waddell's words still ran quietly, full of a persuasive patience.

'Tonight, late—in the Hill House alley,' Spence blurted. Then his voice shrilled. 'But I wouldn't have done it, Marshal! I tell you—I wouldn't. I—I couldn't—!'

Waddell's hand tightened on Spence's thin shoulder. 'Of course not, Spence. You're just not that kind of a man.'

'What—what are you going to do with me?'

'Nothing,' Waddell told him. 'Of course there's the question of the money you took from the cash box. You'll have to straighten that out with your boss, Jack Millerson. I'm turning you over to him.'

This word allayed only part of Spence's fears. 'Geer,' he mumbled. 'And Breed Garvey—they'll be after me. And—'

'I don't think they will,' Waddell broke in. 'But I do want you to keep out of sight until I say different.' Here a faint note of sternness showed.

'He will,' promised Jack Millerson. 'He'll stay in my quarters for a while. You get back there now, Spence. I'll be along presently to talk about things.'

241

Shamed and shaken, Spence Munger got to his feet and shambled out through a rear door. Jack Millerson turned to Waddell. 'Well?'

'I'm halfway sorry for him,' Waddell said.

'A pretty weak specimen for Geer and Garvey to send out to do their dirty work,' Millerson commented. 'You'd thought they'd pick a tougher man.'

'Not necessarily,' Waddell differed briefly. 'Some of the most dangerous men I've ever met with were weak ones, driven frantic by their own fears. It happens that Spence isn't really bad. He evidently took a good look at himself and at what they told him to do, and the decent strain in him revolted.'

'This Rube Kelton,' Millerson asked, 'what about him?'

'He'll be taken care of,' Waddell said.

'And Geer and Garvey?'

'They, too.'

'Ute is a tough street,' Millerson warned.

'Only as tough as it's allowed to be,' Waddell said enigmatically. 'Don't be too rough on Spence Munger. Any idea how much he tapped the till for?'

'Maybe three hundred, from what he admitted.' Millerson scowled uncertainly. 'I don't know exactly what to do about it. I can't bring myself to send him to prison over it, and if I fire him I'll never get any part of it back.'

'Then keep him on and let him work it out,' Waddell suggested. 'From now on he'll probably make you a damn good man.'

He turned to leave and it was Norma Vespasian who hurried to unlock the door for him. For a moment she stood, looking soberly up at him, a warm light in her eyes.

'You're a big man, Chris Waddell,' she said softly. 'For Spence—thanks!'

CHAPTER FOURTEEN

Returning to the office, Chris Waddell paused for a time at the door, marking how far advanced the morning had become and how fully Midas Hill was concerned with this new day. Ore and freight wagons moved ponderously along the street. One of these, creaking under a rich and heavy load of sacked concentrate from the stamp mill, faced the long haul out to the railroad at Decker's Flat. Two armed guards rode with this wagon, one on the box beside the driver, the other perched on the load itself.

On the wide slope past the upper end of Summit Street, the high-lofted sun burned splinters of reflected light in the windows of the various mine and other buildings. Up there at the shaft heads winches were grinding and steel cable squealing in ponderous sheaves. Above engine house exhausts, filaments of steam spurted and trailed. One solid plume of this, rushing whitely, told of a whistle sounding above the mill, and presently this voice, persistent and shrill enough to cut through the solid rumble of the stamps below, reached Waddell.

He turned into the office to again take place in the desk chair. There had been no lessening in the mood which gripped him from the moment he first glimpsed the battered, dead face of Ace MacSwain, nor in his intent toward the brutal killers, or in the extent of it. But another development must be considered now, and full decision reached on it, also.

For the first time, Ute Street had clearly shown its real intent toward him. Ute Street had been set to kill him, this night. In the black gloom of the Hill House alley. The place, the time, the manner, all showed ruthless animal cunning. Ute Street would not kill him within its own limits, thus casting full suspicion on itself. But kill him it would, by one means or another, at some other time, if allowed its way. Which was the solid, ominous fact he now had to consider and work out a full answer to.

There were two alternatives to be faced with grim practicality. Run or fight. One or the other. There was no middle ground. Fight or run! And if he ran, it meant leaving the best part of himself behind—his pride, the vital need of a man's belief in himself. If he fought, then it came down to the brutal truth of kill or be killed. And even should he emerge victor in that, there would be the invisible inner scars for a man to carry all the rest of his years.

He looked down at the badge on his shirt. To a degree it brought to the man wearing it a certain reward in spirit. But also was it a stern taskmaster, which could demand harsh service and on occasion leave its wearer with the gray and somber residue of cruel memories.

He built a cigarette and smoked it slowly. And knew what he had known from the first. He would not run. Regardless of the odds, mental or physical, he must fight.

He smoked his cigarette to the last ash, stubbed it out and went over to the gun rack. He took down the sawed-off shotgun, loaded it and dropped it across his arm. He stepped out into Summit Street, went swiftly along it and turned into Ute.

Down at the lower end of Summit, a rider on a sweating, hard-run horse came to a stop by the corrals. Frank Scorbie stepped from the reeking saddle, and Tim Roach, eyeing the condition of the horse, came around on him angrily.

'You're back before you said you'd be and you punished this animal,' he accused. 'Which teaches me a lesson. Never again do I rent a horse of mine to a damned drunk!'

Scorbie was haggard, his eyes sunken. He even flinched slightly at Roach's words. But his glance was steady and his reply likewise.

'It was a necessity I regret, Tim. But I had to

get here as quickly as I could. Because a man—a damned good man—could be needing me.'

With no further explanation he went past Roach, hurrying.

Chris Waddell's frugal, somewhat enigmatical statement of intent toward Ute Street, just before he left the store, had stayed with Norma Vespasian, and the more she considered it, the more swift and deep grew her concern for him. Her own last remark to him, for all its warmth, had expressed so little of what she really felt and what she really wanted to say. Now, with Jack Millerson out back in his quarters for his understanding with Spence Munger, and with no customers present to demand attention, she turned swiftly to Dad Weyl.

'I'll be back presently, Dad.'

Not waiting reply, she scurried on to the porch and along it, her anxious glance reaching. And saw Waddell emerge from his office, move swiftly to the mouth of Ute Street and swing into it, the shotgun which rested across his arm signifying his intent far more than shouted words might have.

Despite the distance she would have sent a call after him, but he had vanished into Ute before she could voice it. After that she ran, and did not fully realize the uselessness of this until she reached the empty office he had just left. She stopped here, leaning against the door post, her panting breath disturbed and made uneven by sobs of desperation.

A pair of itinerant miners plodded by, to eye her curiously. To get away from this gaze of the street, she turned into the office. The flavor of the cigarette Chris Waddell had so recently smoked in here, still hovered, though serving merely to emphasize the emptiness of the room.

She had only partly recovered and was still dabbing at her eyes, when the sunlight at the open door was partly blotted out by the figure of Frank Scorbie. He exclaimed, staring at her, marking her upset manner.

'Miss Vespasian! What is it? There's something wrong?'

Her first impulse was to storm at this man, to flay him, to charge him with the guilt of drunkenness and cowardice and of selling out his badge of office. And of leaving another man to take on responsibilities and risks which were rightfully his. But she did not. Instead, she gave him the word quite simply.

'It's Chris—Chris Waddell. Last night they brutally murdered a good friend of his. They had planned the same for him this coming night. So now—now he's gone down Ute Street after them—alone—!'

Frank Scorbie was silent for a single long moment. Then he made steady statement.

'Not alone. No, he won't be alone!'

He was out of the room as quickly as he had

entered.

Chris Waddell's first stop was the Staghorn. It was too early in the day for much activity on Ute Street; at this hour the street was mainly occupied in sleeping off its excesses of the previous night. In the Staghorn, only two were present. Neither was Breed Garvey, the man behind the bar being a new face to Waddell.

The other, he knew. A roan-headed, narrow-faced, lank-mustached person who no longer carried one-arm in a sling, though continuing to favor it. He stood at the end of the bar, slouched over a drink. At Waddell's entrance he turned statue-still, staring straight ahead.

Waddell shot his abrupt question at the bartender. 'Garvey—where is he?'

He saw the beginning of a lie build in the bartender's eyes, so he shifted the shotgun slightly. The bartender blinked and made careful reply.

'Seems I remember him sayin' somethin' about the Belle Union.'

'Remarkable memory,' Waddell observed sarcastically. 'Don't lose it.'

He shifted the shotgun again, putting the twin muzzle roughly in line with the roan-headed one at the end of the bar.

'You—Kelton!'

The words seemed to possess physical force, the way they brought Rube Kelton around, strain settling in his eyes and tightening his

248

cheeks.

'You want to try it now?' Waddell challenged.

'Try—what?' Kelton's words were dry and cautious.

'What you figured to do tonight in case Spence Munger missed me!'

The tension in Kelton's cheeks deepened and wariness cloaked him like it might an animal. 'I still don't get it,' he blurted.

'The hell you don't!' charged Waddell. 'Now see if you can understand this. Get out of town! I'll be coming back this way presently. Don't let me find you anywhere around. That's it, Kelton. Head for new country—and don't come back! My final word!'

Rube Kelton watched him leave, then turned to the bartender.

'Now there's a hell of a nerve. Him trying to give me a floater!'

'He didn't just try,' corrected the bartender bluntly. 'He did give you one.'

'Hell with him!' blustered Kelton. 'I won't leave.'

The bartender shrugged and dispensed further wisdom.

'Your funeral. And that's what it will be.'

Rube Kelton turned back to his drink and downed it while brooding over this pungent and disquieting statement. Abruptly he wheeled to the door.

'So long!' he said.

From the Staghorn, Chris Waddell headed directly for the Belle Union, and Frank Scorbie, turning into Ute Street, glimpsed that high, quick striding figure and broke into a run. Passing in front of the Staghorn, Scorbie collided with a man just emerging from the place.

The lighter of the two, Rube Kelton came near being upset, and he snarled angrily as he straightened. But the snarl died quickly at what he read in Frank Scorbie's expression and when Scorbie rushed on, Rube Kelton went the other way, his own steps hurrying.

In the Belle Union, Evie Spooner was seated at a poker table, making very late breakfast on stale remnants left from last night's free lunch, and washing them down with a couple of whiskies. Lee Spooner was still at the free lunch shelf, selecting his choice before joining his brother. The barkeep on duty paid them no attention, used to them having free run of the place. Thus were these three placed when Chris Waddell entered.

He came steadily along the room to stop across the poker table from Elvie Spooner. He thumbed a worn and twisted silver dollar from a pocket and dropped it in front of Elvie.

'Yours, I believe!'

Elvie rested his hands against the edge of the table, switching his hard glance from Waddell to the coin, then back to Waddell again. 'Who says it's mine?' he demanded.

'Men who have seen it on you. It was picked up where Ace MacSwain was found, beat to death. Spooner, for that I'm going to see you hung!'

Snake fast, Elvie Spooner shoved the table at Waddell, upsetting it against him. At the same moment he yelled warning.

'Lee—look out!'

On the heels of the yell, Frank Scorbie came in from the street.

Alert as he had been for trouble, Waddell could not avoid the drive of the table and the impact knocked him to one knee, which caused Lee Spooner to miss him with a bullet that cut through just above his head. Cursing, Lee was ready to chop down for a second try when Waddell turned the shotgun loose, its roaring blast completely soaking up the echoes of Lee's shot.

The charge of buckshot was a wicked, deadly, close-packed hail of lead which raked the side and top of the bar and in part caught Lee full in the face. He died instantly as four of the lead pellets chewed through his narrow skull.

Still on one knee, Waddell emptied the second barrel into the top of the poker table, guessing at the angle and guessing wrong. For the charge, though blasting a hole through the table top and scattering a burst of splinters beyond, could not spread at this close range and so narrowly missed Elvie Spooner who was whirling to one side, dragging a gun.

He had this fully on Waddell when from the other end of the room another gun challenged, driving hard, rolling report and a bullet which caught Elvie full in the center of the chest, heart-high. It locked him in instant paralysis, spun him around and dropped him on his face.

It had been sudden, it had been explosive, it had been savage. In less than a dozen breaths, two men who had chosen to live violently, had so died. The bartender stood frozen, stupid. Frank Scorbie, advancing down the room with the gun that had just dropped Elvie Spooner, ready in his hand, tipped the weapon significantly. The bartender did not miss the hint. He spread both hands palm down on the mahogany and held them so, breathing hard through his nose.

The belting pound of the shots had poured their racket all through the building. In the back room, after the first long moment of stunned silence which followed the gunfire, there came a rush of movement, the door banged open and bursting through came Hogan Geer, with Price Ringgold and Breed Garvey pushing at his heels.

Hogan Geer came to such an abrupt stop the others bumped into him, shoving him half around. He stayed that way, staring. At his feet lay Lee Spooner, twisted and dead. Yonder, face down by an upset poker table, Elvie Spooner lay. Also by that poker table was

Chris Waddell, just coming erect again, discarding the empty shotgun and drawing his belt weapon. And coming up even with Waddell was Frank Scorbie, cold sober and level eyed, fisting a drawn gun.

'Things have changed, Geer,' said Frank Scorbie. 'Now you crawl!'

Hogan Geer was too shrewd a man, too much a fatalist not to understand what this meant. He might plot, he might contrive, he might play a sly and treacherous game—but he had never tried to beguile himself by refusing to face realities. And with the chips down he was a far tougher man than any of those he maneuvered to his bidding. He proved it now, by coming up with a snub-snouted pocket gun of heavy caliber and drilling a slug which cut between Waddell's left arm and his body, barely flicking the arm with the searing touch of a red hot iron. Then he was knocked back and down by Waddell's and Scorbie's almost simultaneous shots.

Breed Garvey was apparently unarmed; at any rate he made no try for a weapon. He just stood, hunched forward, glowering like some burly animal about to charge, but held immobile by the threat of Frank Scorbie's gun and his harsh:

'Don't try it, Garvey!'

It was Price Ringgold who really turned craven. This sneering, arrogant, sardonic fellow, this tawny one with his pale eyes and feline fastidiousness, broke completely in the face of stark, brutal reality. He flung his hands up even with his ears and came forward, exclaiming.

'No!—no! Don't shoot—don't shoot—!'

Neither Chris Waddell nor Frank Scorbie had further intention that way unless forced to it. But now it was Hogan Geer, huddled and dying on the floor, who struggled to one elbow, mumbled thickly.

'No you don't, by God! You went into this with me, you go out—with me!'

Saying which, and before Waddell or Scorbie could do anything about it, Geer brought up his snub-nosed gun and shot Ringgold between the shoulders.

Then Geer fell back and was still.

Silence came down, reeking with the bitter incense of gunsmoke and the invisible winds of death. Breed Garvey swayed from side to side, bearlike, locked in ponderous uncertainty. It was Frank Scorbie who broke the wire-tight stillness.

'You heard what I told Geer, Breed. Things have changed. Like Geer, you've been around Midas Hill too long. You've sold too much rot-gut liquor and you've robbed and rolled too many drunks. So you got to make a choice. Either you leave these hills, or—you take the consequences. It's a better break than you deserve. What's it to be?'

Garvey did not even hesitate. 'I'll leave,' he

said hoarsely.

*   *   *

The afternoon was well along. Blue and lavender haze leaked off the higher ridges and flowed down in long ripples of shadow, slowly chasing sunlight from the town.

In the office, Chris Waddell sat alone, awaiting the slow emergence of renewed spirit. A great weariness held him and all the processes of his mind seemed warped and shriveled. He hardly stirred when Frank Scorbie and Doc Stone came in together. Doc was carrying his satchel and he slapped this down on the desk, opened it, and after a bit of rummaging, came up with a sealed pint.

'I've seen my roughest day,' he growled. 'And I need a real slug of this. You got some glasses handy, Scorbie?'

'Why yes,' Scorbie answered. 'There should be some.'

He produced three and Doc poured, generously. Scorbie pushed Waddell's glass across to him, then met Waddell's sharpening glance and read his doubting thought.

'Just this one, Chris,' he said quietly. 'For me there never again will be more than one.'

Waddell came to his feet, his eyes clearing and turning warm.

'Why Frank—we'll drink on that!'

Doc repacked his bag, rumbling his

255

reflective thoughts.

'It's happened before—it will happen again. The wrong kind never learn that there is always a price to pay. It sure has been one hell of a day!'

With that he downed the balance of his drink and went away.

Waddell spoke slowly. 'Yes, a hell of a day. I want no more of such. I'm taking off the badge, Frank—for good.'

'I can understand why you would feel that way just now,' Scorbie said carefully. 'But in a week or two—?'

Waddell shook his head. 'Not in a year or two. Not ever.' He unpinned the badge from his shirt, laid it on the desk. 'That's it. Today is my day to call it quits. I know it in my head, I know it in my heart. I've walked down my last Ute Street. I want no more of them.' He took a short turn up and down the office. 'I'm at a spot in the trail where I'll never be again. I make the break now, or never. And it is now!' He paused by Scorbie and dropped a hand on his shoulder.

'You saved my life back there, Frank. Elvie Spooner had me dead to rights. It will be a good thought to carry with me—and the knowledge that you and I, we made one final walk down a tough street—together. Yes, that is good. And it is extra good to know that while I lost one good friend last night in Ace MacSwain, I regained an old one today when I needed him most. Yes, this is the time to step out!'

Scorbie mused for a moment, recalling the things he had seen in Norma Vespasian's eyes when she stood in this office and sent him to Chris Waddell's aid. Slowly he nodded.

'You're looking ahead to better things which I never could hope to see, Chris. Yeah, looking further and seeing better. So the best of it all to you.'

*   *   *

In the purple twilight he waited by the door of Jack Millerson's store, and when she came out, he took her arm.

'I would walk you home, Norma.'

She was grave and subdued. Presently Waddell added:

'Frank Scorbie told me how you directed him to find me. If you hadn't done that, I wouldn't be here now.'

She shivered and pressed closer to him. 'It—it must have been terrible—in the Belle Union.'

'Yes,' he agreed, 'it was. But it will not happen again with me. I've taken off the badge, for good.'

They turned into the Hill House alley and went along it. In the clearing beyond, Norma slowed.

'What will you do, Chris?'

'Cattle. The old call is back again. But first I'd like to ride the hills with you.'

In the dusk her eyes took on a soft shining.

'There are a lot of trails. And I know them all.'